YOU

SADIE BLACK

Copyright © 2016 Sadie Black

All rights reserved.

DEDICATION

For Sophia…

Chapter One

The sun descending over Incheon International airport left Jun Tae Min's heart feeling as if it carried the world. He couldn't remember another time when his heart beat so slowly. Perhaps it was only in his head, but Jun Tae couldn't shake the sensation. At times it got so strong, he didn't know what to do with the pain of it all. The helplessness at the turn his life had taken left him so frustrated, the urge to cry raged through him for he was out of options. Then again, he spent a week and a half sobbing in a corner in a filthy hotel room, a far cry from where he'd been mere weeks before. He had climbing the musical charts, being shown on ever music station in Asia and his video for his newest release, *Salang,* had been playing almost constantly on MNET. Then with three words, with one simple sentence that shouldn't be that important, the whole country turned its back on him.

The pilot gave the usual speech and the hostesses did the usual explanation of safety procedures. He glanced around and as always, no one was really paying attention. They'd sat through that same demonstration so many time, it had lost all meaning over time. Jun Tae wondered why they did that to begin with for if the plane was to crash, in panic, no one would remember anything they'd pantomimed.

The moment they were finished, the plane gently lurched forward and continued down the runway before it shot off into the sky. He never liked flying on the best of days but he had to get away from Korea, from the place that had betrayed him in ways that left him confused and numb.

Rubbing his eyes, he looked down into the bank book and took a breath. Fourteen point eight million dollars in a Canadian account. Thankfully his parent's dual citizenship came in handy. He was able to go to University in Toronto, fast track through his Literature program and graduated, at the top of his class, with a B.A in English Literature. During that time he worked gigs around the city, being featured at the Toronto Kpop Convention and had some success there. What money he made, he was able to open a bank account and stashed it away there. Though he could have become a teacher back in his home land of South Korea,

Jun Tae followed his dreams to become a Kpop star.

Taking a deep breath, he closed the book and shoved it into his carryon bag, then slid it under his seat. The flight back to Toronto would be a long one so he might as well get some sleep.

But his rest didn't last long. The hostess came around to ask if he would like something from the overflowing, silver cart she pushed along the aisle. He hadn't had a chance to eat for a few hours but just the thought of putting food in his mouth made him ill. He smiled at her, fairly certain she didn't recognized him for he was going under his real name—not just JT Min as he was known all over Korea. Plus he bleached his hair to a bright blond, almost white colour. He accepted a glass of wine along with some grapes and settled back in the seat.

The flight slithered on and on. He switched planes in San Francisco and Chicago before landing at Pearson International. By then, he was exhausted and just wanted to go to his hotel and crash. They didn't ask him as many question for he was travelling under his Canadian passport. As the agent welcomed him back, Jun Tae said a silent prayer he'd kept renewing his passport over the years, that he wasn't one of those people who refused to keep it going because they feel as if he was betraying their country. His parents were born in Canada and with their citizenship intact, they ensured he had his as well.

Thankfully, June was one of the warmer months in Toronto and when he stepped outside, his body instantly began defrosting from the artificial air. For a moment, he merely stood there, eyes closed, fingers of one hand gripping the handle to his suite case and the fingers from the other holding the straps to his carryon. He lifted his face to the sun and exhaled long and hard. The smell of Toronto was different—a mixture of vehicles and spices from a nearby hotdog stand. But there was something else—he inhaled deeply, held the breath then exhaled—freedom.

Someone bounced into him and he opened his eyes and took a step to the side to allow a crowd of people to get by him then walked along the sidewalk to the taxi stand. The shuttle bus for his hotel pulled to a stop behind the cab but he didn't feel like dealing with people. After climbing into the back seat, he told the driver the address then lounged back in the seat. Jun Tae knew someone who smoked had occupied the vehicle before he did. The stale stench of cigarettes wafted off the leather around him.

The car made its way from the maze that was highway exits and entrances of the Airport area and into the downtown Toronto core. He leaned forward, almost pressing his forehead against the window to take in the high towers of glass monstrosities. Tall buildings weren't foreign to him by any means, but no matter how many times he witnessed them, they still had a certain allure.

The hotel sat amongst office buildings, theatres and along a street that was lined on the opposite side with restaurants. He couldn't help smirking at one that had the bum of a fiber glass cow sticking out one part of the building and the head out another. Jun Tae paid his driver and rolled his suitcase into the building. A smartly dressed man tipped his hat at Jun Tae and opened the glass doors for him.

"Thanks," Jun Tae said with a grin.

Inside he checked in and was escorted to his suite by another cleanly dressed man—younger man this time who wasn't particularly handsome. He had a crooked nose and an untrustworthy grin. His hair seemed as if it was trying to be curly but was cut far too short and the neck of his shirt was as though it cut off circulation. Still, Jun Tae tipped him and closed his door to take in the space around him.

Jun Tae was finally in the silence of his own space, free to wallow in what self pity he had left. He ventured deeper into the room, leaving his bag by the bedroom door. He found the phone and after consulting the guide beside it, he called room service and ordered a cheese pizza. While he waited, he found what was in the mini-bar, poured himself a drink and peeled his shirt off. Once he was somewhat comfortable, he grabbed his cell phone, scrolled through the names and hit send.

The ringing on the other end unnerved him more than he thought possible. He wasn't used to waiting so long for his friend to pick up—at least he hoped Carson was still his friend. The two had parted ways on good terms and had stayed in contact until the proverbial shit hit the proverbial fan weeks prior. Everyone else was gone—now he waited. Why would Carson still want him around anyway? Jun Tae knew he brought nothing but bad luck lately and what if Carson didn't want that in his life.

"Hello?"

"Um—Carson?"

"JT?"

Jun Tae's heart fluttered. "Yeah. How are you?"

"Forget how I am," Carson said. "I saw the

report on MNET about the drama happening with you. How are *you?* Are you safe? Where are you? Want me to fly in to Korea? We could hook up on Seoul man and I can get you out, you don't even have to worry."

Tears tumbled down Jun Tae's cheeks then. He wasn't even sure when he'd started crying. He held his breath. "I'm in Toronto."

"How?"

"Remember how I told you my parents were Canadians?"

"Oh right! That's good! Where are you then?"

Jun Tae gave Carson his address.

"Stay there. I'm coming over."

"Carson you…"

But Carson was gone and all remained of him was the echoes of the dial tone.

Jun Tae called the room service again and

added to his order. He knew Carson hated cheese pizza so he got a second one with pepperoni and ground beef, along with a few sodas, a case of six beers and chicken wings.

As usual, Carson showed up the same time the room service server was rolling the food tray into the room. After tipping him, Jun Tae stood before Carson and tilted his head not sure if he should hug him or shake his hand. Carson was still massive in size and the smile on his handsome face hadn't shrunken in the two years he hadn't seen the man personally. Standing at an overpowering six foot three, with muscles for days, Carson was the kind of man that could break you in all the best ways in his bed. He had to be.

Carson hugged him tightly. "I was worried."

"I didn't mean to do that," Jun Tae said. "I

came out to my parents and the world ended."

"I'm sorry brother."

"Still?"

Carson stepped back. This time, his large lips curved upward in a frown. "What's that supposed to mean?"

"It means—you still want to be my friend even after the mess I've made of everything? Even after—you know?"

"Look, you didn't make a mess." Carson sounded indignant. "You took the next logical step in your life and a few people lost their damn minds like you stripped naked in front of them and their kids. Don't carry that guilt with you. Let it go."

"I can't. You called me *brother* and I want to make sure you still wish to be my friend."

"Look man, when I was in school with you, you always had my back," Carson said. "You helped me when no one else would, you cared. You sat up with me all night so I can pass the dumb French as a Second Language course when you didn't have to. I'm not about to repay kindness with pain. That's not me. So you're gay. Who cares? Who you sleep with is none of my business—well unless he's an asshole then he and I would have a conversation—well, he and my fists—but you get what I mean."

"Thank you."

"For what? I'm very comfortable in my manhood. I don't need to hate on others to feel big."

"Still—thank you. Okay, let's eat and we can talk about this."

The two sat down over their meals and reminisced of old times. Soon, however, the talk went to what Jun Tae was planning on doing with the rest of his life. Sure, he could go back to Korea, but there was nothing there for him. His parents and brother had all disowned him, so he was alone in the world.

"I see this as a blessing, you know?" Carson said.

Jun Ta arched a brow. "Oh yeah? How?"

"Well, you're always saying how you hated the bubblegum crap they were making you sing," Carson replied. "Now you can do your own music—what you want to do."

Jun Tae leaned back in his chair and expelled a loud breath through his mouth. He then bit into a slice of pizza and chewed thoughtfully. "I could." He supposed. "But what the hell kind of style does my music have? Any suggestions?"

"First, stop insinuating about sex," Carson advised. "You're a grown-ass man. Call it what it is. You're gay, own it. No more of these weird videos where a strange couple roll around in a bed and you sing looking out a window—none of that crap. Make the sensual videos you want to make with what you're into."

"I don't know about all that."

Carson grinned. "Good for you that you have me and I know. Listen, brother, there's a pretty big Kpop scene here now. Thanks to Gerald Butler and the guys over at Pop! Goes the World. Why don't you reach out to them? Wait, before you do that. I know a guy who owns a club downtown. It's in Korea town. I could make a few calls and see if he'll let you do a few gigs there—build up your name again."

"I don't know yet." Jun Tae shoved a piece of pizza into his mouth and chewed slowly. "I don't have any new materials and due to copyrights I can't use what I have so far.

Honestly, I want to distance myself as much as I can from that name."

"That's another talk for another time with more booze," Carson said. "Well, maybe you can take some time and think about it. Put some ink on paper with new material and I can hook you up. My studio has some free time coming up in a couple of weeks, if you want it, it's yours."

"How much?"

"Don't be a dope, huh JT?" Carson frowned, his beautiful brown, eyes darkening. "You can thank me by putting me one of your videos."

"Um—since you say I should own being gay, chances are the video will have gay content—you know that."

Carson laughed. "It's all acting, brother! Anyone can do that. As long as it's not—like—

porn."

Jun Tae laughed and held up his beer. "To new beginnings and a great friend."

"I will drink to that, brother." Carson touched his bottle to Jun Tae's and then drank.

Chapter Two

"Ma?" Fynn Gibbs let himself through the front door and into a luxurious foyer. He craned his neck to look up the winding staircase of polished mahogany with the black banister to see if he could catch sight of his mother. "Ma, you here?"

He removed his shoes, set them on the mat by the door and wandered further into the house. The corridor wall was line with pictures of himself and his mother and father ever since he was a child until he became an adult. His mother had always had a thing for family photos.

He found his mother in the kitchen, a strange place a billionaire's wife but Paulette loved the act of cooking. She always told him one of the kindest thing a mother and a wife can do was cook for her husband and children. It was weird to her having a stranger make their meals.

Truth be told she was very good at cooking and baking. When Fynn got hurt doing a trick at a dance competition a year before, his mother took him home and helped nurse him back to health. He couldn't dance or hit the gym with a busted ankle so he gained eighteen pounds eating her food.

"Hey, Ma," he said.

She turned, surprise on her face. "Trix!" She greeted him with his nickname. She'd given it to him as a baby because he would always find a way to climb out of his crib—she couldn't figure out how he did it. To her, according to what Paulette had told him, Fynn was her little Houdini full of tricks. "I didn't hear you come in. You're early."

"Yeah. Had to cancel one of my classes tonight because the equipment wasn't working. How are you?"

"In my day we didn't have any of that fancy gadget crap," she said. "It was the teacher, a black chalk board, white chalk and nothing else."

Fynn smiled.

"Taste this pasta sauce and tell me what it's missing." She lifted the spoon toward him.

"Um—sure." He tasted from the spoon she lifted toward him and tilted his head. "Oregano and ground pepper."

"Hrm." She mused.

He kissed the side of her head and grabbed an apple from the pile on the island. Wiping it in his shirt, he took a bite.

"Hey, were you raised by bears?" Paulette asked. "You're supposed wash that first. And you're going to ruin your appetite!"

"No I won't." Fynn grinned at her. "I could eat a cow right now and still have dinner—I'm that hungry."

She waved the spoon at him. Fynn laughed and took another bite from the fruit.

"I thought Carson was supposed to join us tonight for dinner."

"He was." Fynn crunched through the flesh of the apple again and moaned. "But a friend of his is going through some stuff right now. He went off to see if he can help."

"I told you he was a good sort," Paulette said. She turned her attention to dicing an onion. she didn't speak until after she'd dropped the pieces into her sauce. "I always liked it."

"Yeah, I figure I'd keep him. Besides, selling him on ebay is illegal."

Paulette laughed at the joke.

"Where's Dad?"

"Last minute meeting at the office. He should be here around seven-ish. You don't have a performance tonight, do you?"

"No. It's just strange he isn't home."

"Well, he has to figure out the Christmas flavours for this year. The labs are already riding him about it."

"I thought he wasn't going to do that anymore?" Fynn asked. "He always complains about how much work it is and how much pressure he gets under to pick something everyone will like."

"You know your father. Help me by setting the table, would you son?"

"Sure." Fynn took a final bite of the fruit and tossed the pit into the garbage. He then washed his hands, dried them in the hem of his mom's apron before grabbing plates, wine glasses along with knives and forks. He carried them in a pile to the table and began working. "Ma, I meant to talk to you about something."

"Sounds serious."

"It kind of is." Fynn set a plate where his father usually sits for family dinners. "Remember the day I told you I was gay?"

"Of course. *Ma, listen, I don't like, like girls.*" She reminisced.

"You and dad didn't freak out. I'm glad you didn't but I'm curious."

Paulette chuckled. "It's not like it was any secret. Your father and I knew."

"You did? How?"

"Come on, Trix. You were fifteen and never once did you bring home a girl. I never heard you talking about a girl you liked, or a girl you thought was hot and you paid more attention to Captain Von Trapp in the *Sound of Music* than you did Maria or the countess."

Fynn laughed. "Thanks, Ma. Judge my sexuality based on a movie."

"Sorry. But seriously, we knew. You weren't girly or anything like that. There was just something about you that told us. Your father and I talked about it and we agreed."

"Why didn't you say something?" Fynn wandered back to the kitchen to grab juice glasses for his design at the dinner table. "Do you know how freaked out I was to tell you and dad?"

"I'm sorry you were worried, darling. But

what should we have said?" Paulette turned to face him then. "It wasn't foolproof, Trix. It was a thought and though we both saw something, we could've been wrong. Besides, we figured you'd come to us when you were ready. In the mean time, we read the books, spoke to a shrink—we never once thought against loving you. We just wanted to handle it properly because we've seen so many LGBT youths get lost in the world because their parents react the exact wrong way."

Fynn nodded.

"I'm not saying one hundred percent of parents should be okay with it one hundred percent of the time right out the gate," Paulette carried on. "It is a lot to take in knowing your daughter or your son isn't *normal.* I know, that's a horrible way to put it but it is the truth. We don't care for normal. I'm saying in this case, you are our son. And you've never once disappointed us. We couldn't stop loving you if we tried—gay or not. We just had to switch our thinking from having a daughter in law to a son in law and maybe adopted grand-children. Our love for you outweighs all the other petty crap, you know?"

Fynn sighed and hugged his mom tightly. He rubbed her back then dropped a chaste kiss to her lips. "I love you, Ma. I mean that."

She looked up into his gaze, her eyes shimmering happily. "I know you do. Your father and I were talking last night about how proud we are of you." Paulette stepped from his arms to pull a couple packs of pasta from the cupboard.

"What for?"

"First, you're our son. Second, you're living a life that you can be proud of, and third, instead of sitting at home and depending on your father's money, you're making your own—slowly—but surely."

"It isn't my money, Ma. And it feels good to make some of my own."

"When was the last time you touched your trust fund?"

Fynn couldn't remember. He'd been booking more and more gigs lately and was even asked to be a contract creative writing professor at one of the local colleges. That he accepted the minute he got the offer package. He was one of the youngest professors at the college and got the job because of his degree in Creative Writing and his numerous published pieces in different journals all over Canada. "About a year now?"

"See what I mean? You know Boris Anderson's son?"

"Petrov? Yeah."

"Dropped out of Cal Tech with eight months left to graduate," Paulette explained. "Can you believe that fool? Now he's living in Dubai on daddy's dime, racing sports cars for free."

"That makes no sense. It's only eight months to go. I mean, he got through, what? Three years before that? And if you're going to endanger your life at least risk it for a reason."

"That was the exact point I made to your father." Paulette tsked. "All I'm trying to make you understand is that you're a great son."

Fynn's cheeks heated and he bowed his head. It'd been a while since he'd had such an in-depth talk with his mother. He felt it was long overdue especially after he saw the way one of his student's parents reacted to her being a lesbian. It wasn't good but she wasn't letting that get the better of her. She was in his class, fighting to follow her dreams to become an author. From what he read so far of her stuff, she was good—hell, better than good. She wrote some things he wished he was mature enough to come up with.

His father, Denny, got home a little later than expected so they had dinner together about nine at night. Fynn stuck around to help his mother wash the dishes before retiring to his father's office to sit around watching episodes of *Outlander.* Fynn never got why his father loved the show—he understood why his mother liked it since Jamie wasn't bad on the eyes. And apparently that accent made the ladies go crazy, but Fynn was never a Scottish accent kind of lover. Give him an Irish or a Spanish accent any day.

"I thought Carson was supposed to be here

tonight," Denny said, taking a sip from his glass.

"Yeah. He had a friend with an emergency."

"Oh. I hope everything is all right."

"Me too. I'm going to catch up with him tomorrow before my first class. I guess he'll tell me if he can."

"I wanted to talk to you about something," Denny said. He glanced toward the door as though to make sure they were still alone. "You know how your mother and my wedding anniversary is coming up?"

Fynn nodded.

"I was thinking of taking her somewhere— a trip. What do you think of a Mediterranean cruise?"

Fynn arched a surprise brow. "But, dad, you hate the waves."

"I know. But she's always wanted to go on one. And it wouldn't be much of an anniversary cruise if I paid for it and she went alone or with Margie. I can get over it for a few days with her."

"Then I like the idea. Is this a surprise?"

Denny nodded with a proud grin. "I have to call Bev so she can make the reservations."

"Great idea. I could keep an eye on the old place while you're away, no problem."

"Thanks son." He drained the rest of his bourbon and set the glass on a coaster on the desk. "I've been meaning to ask you this, and don't take it the wrong way."

"O-Kay. Shoot."

"Shouldn't you be dating?"

Fynn almost choked on his inhaled breath. "Um…What?"

"Since you were nineteen we haven't

seen you really go out with anyone," Denny pointed out. "I mean, you're a good looking guy."

"Well—er—I don't date as much anymore. With men I can't figure out if they want me for me or the Gibbs name and what comes with that."

"Dang—sorry, son."

"It's not a problem." Fynn shook his head. "You and ma worked hard to give me a life and this name. There's no shame in it—nothing to apologize for."

"I know. It's…I don't want you to be lonely."

Fynn smiled. "I'm not going to lie, sometimes it does get lonely. But, I have my teaching and my writing and my dancing—my life is pretty full right now. I guess if I ever meet someone worthy then I'll bring them home but not before."

"Good thought."

Fynn exhaled long and hard.

"Now." Denny said. "Your old man isn't as young as he used to be. I'm going to take a shower and crawl into bed."

"I should head home," Fynn said. He rose and hugged his father. "I love you, dad."

"Love you too. Don't leave without saying goodbye to your mother."

Fynn promised he wouldn't and after accepting a kiss to the side of his head from his father, he fell into his vacated chair again and stretched his legs out before him. For a silent moment he sat there, thinking how lucky had to be. He didn't know what he would have done if his parents had freaked out like most others.

After saying bye to his mother, and accepting a doggie bag for Carson, he slipped into the leather seat of his BMW and turned for home. On his way he stopped at Carson's place and called his friend's cell.

"Hey, brother!" Carson answered. "How was dinner with the parents?"

"Great. Ma made pasta."

"With those turkey meatballs?"

"You guessed it."

Carson groaned. "Oh man."

"Don't fret, man. She sent you some." Fynn told him. "You home?"

"No. I'm still at my friend's hotel. Um—you wanna swing by here?"

"Nah." Fynn started the ignition to his car again but didn't pull it from park. "I'll take it home and drop it in the fridge. You can pick it up from me tomorrow when I see you at the gym."

"Perfect. You don't mind if I bring JT, do

you?"

"You said he was going through a hard time, right?"

"Yeah."

"Not a good time for anyone to be alone." Fynn told him. "Bring him."

"You rule, Trix. I swear to God. See you tomorrow."

Fynn laughed and hung up. He glanced in his mirror, switched the vehicle to drive and pulled from the curb. It was probably for the best anyway. When he and Carson got together, the world could end and neither of them wouldn't know it.

Chapter Three

After a quick stop with Carson at a nearby clothing store, Jun Tae felt a little bit more prepared for the gym. They drove there in silence, for he was already going over in his head lyrics to a song he'd been trying to make come together before putting it on paper. He had the melody ready and a thought he could use a rapper in it as well but that was as far as he got.

And where the hell was he going to find a rapper to pen a duet with some washed up Kpop singer?

Jun Tae felt ill.

The gym was a sprawling one in the middle of downtown. Glass walls at the front exposed people jogging on treadmills with their headphones in. He figured they just looked like a bunch of dummies running like crazy but not actually going anywhere.

It seemed Carson knew everyone. By the time they got to the front doors, they'd stopped so many times and Carson had introduced Jun Tae to so many people, Jun Tae lost track. Finally, Jun Tae thought they were in the clear until Carson met someone else he knew and Jun Tae excused himself so they could have a talk. Jun Tae allowed himself inside and was instantly bombarded with the sounds of a gym—machines, televisions blaring, someone's music playing too loud for their headphones. But what really drew him was the call of a coach to the two men in a ring to the far right side. They were doing mixed martial arts, something Jun Tae always admired but never had the courage to try.

The coach forced both men to release each other and stand. Jun Tae took a good look at all three. Coach was your typical white male, overly gray hair with a pudgy belly. Jun Tae knew he had an origin story—a reason he was the man the fighters chose to lead them. One of the fighters looked as if he'd taken one too many shots to the face and head. His face was heavily scarred and his ears were like oversized cauliflowers. He had blond hair, tied back in a neat ponytail, a tattoo of a giant lizard down his spine and the word *Warrior* was carved into his back from one shoulder tip to the next.

The other man was dark skinned, looked tall maybe about six feet and handsome. His straight nose wasn't too long or pudgy and it wasn't crooked to Jun Tae's pleasure. The man's brown eyes were intense as they latched onto his opponent and led down to thick, full lips that were pursed almost as if in thought. He didn't have a hint of a tattoo anywhere—though Jun Tae knew it could be under the *Affliction* shirt he wore. Jun Tae found himself wondering what it would be like to find out, to explore this man's body until he knew everything about it—it's curves, its scars, its blemishes—everything.

He shook his head and continued watching the sparring. The dark skinned man had muscles like a swimmer, lean and tight. That was the kind of body Jun Tae found himself attracted to. Clearing his throat, he went as close as he could and kept his eyes fused to the chocolate stud.

I would do things to that man and his body

that shouldn't be legal.

Carson tapped him on the shoulder and Jun Tae looked away from the scene as if he was caught with his hand in the cookie jar. His friend then turned his goofy grin to the men in the ring.

"Yo! Trix!" Carson shouted. "You started without me?"

The African American male in the ring held up a hand to stop the sparring and walked over to smile down at Carson. His teeth, Jun Tae noticed, were just as perfect as the rest o f him.

"You were taking way too long," Trix said. "You haven't even changed."

"I know." Carson smirked. "I wanted to introduce my friend Jun Tae Min. JT, this is Fynn Gibbs."

Fynn extended a gloved hand. Jun Tae

accepted and shook after wiping his palms against his thighs.

"It's nice to meet you," Fynn said.

"Same here."

"Okay you two, go change. I rented a private space for us so once you're in proper attire…" Fynn grinned. "We can begin."

"Begin?" Jun Tae asked, following Carson. "Beging what?"

"Fynn Gibbs is a taskmaster in the gym," Carson said. "We're in for an hour of pure hell."

Jun Tae groaned. It'd been a while since he'd seriously hit the gym. Usually he ran or danced to get his heart going. Still, he wasn't about to be embarrassed in front of Fynn, no way was that going to happen.

But that was easier said than done. Halfway through the first set of burpees, Jun

Tae wanted to die.

Though Fynn told him to speak up if he needed to stop, Jun Tae gritted his teeth and soldiered through. He went up into an handstand and walked to the second set of burpees like Fynn and Carson had. When the routine was over, he fell to his back and swore he was passing in and out of consciousness. He hadn't been that exhausted in—in—ever.

"I think I'm dying," Jun Tae admitted. "Was that a military course or something? I mean, I didn't get drunk and sign up to join the Canadian Forces, did I?"

"No," Fynn said with a chuckle.

Jun Tae looked up into his handsome, sweat covered face. "No? So you mean you do that all the time? For fun?"

Fynn smirked. "I told you to let me know if you wanted to stop."

"You do that for *fun*?" Jun Tae repeated his question. "*All* the time?"

"Yeah. You have to build up your muscles," Fynn told him. "Besides, you got through it without dying. You may be tired but you're alive."

Jun Tae tried sitting up but only succeeded he falling to his back again. "That's still up for debate. I can't feel my left big toe"

"You're just being dramatic." Carson laughed. "You haven't felt anything yet. Wait until tomorrow morning. You'll be hurting in places you never knew exists."

Jun Tae groaned.

Fynn laughed. "He's exaggerating."

"So I won't be in any pain?" Jun Tae asked.

"Oh, I didn't say all that." Fynn replied proudly. "You'll be in pain, all right."

Carson sat up. "Told you."

"That's not something to be proud of!" Jun Tae eyed Carson with a frown.

"Once you've done it a few times, you'll be used to it." Fynn nodded. "Your muscles won't be asleep anymore and you can do other things."

"Oh no," Jun Tae pushed to his bum, shaking his head. "I'm not falling for that again. No more boot camp sessions for me."

"You're Korean. Didn't you have to do two years of military service?" Fynn asked. "You should be used to this."

"Yeah about that—I'm technically Canadian," Jun Tae Said. "Parents have dual citizenship. My brother and I were born here—long story. Carson, help me up, would you? I don't think my muscles can stand the push to my feet."

"Here." Fynn stood and extended a hand.

For a breath, Jun Tae hesitated. Then he caught himself, licked his lips and offered Fynn his hand. With a strong tug, Jun Tae was on his feet and quickly took his hand back. "Thanks." He rubbed his lower back. "I'm going to need a massage."

"Fynn gives a great back massage," Carson said, fiddling with his laces. "He's got magical fingers."

"Oh no!" Jun Tae shook his head. "No thank you. I'm not letting Attila the Hun here do anything else to my body."

Fynn and Carson laughed out loud. Jun Tae only frowned and headed for the showers.

♥

Fynn stared a Jun Tae's retreating back

until he disappeared behind the heavy doors of the change room. It took him a while to realize he had been staring. But Jun Tae had a strong back and strangely wide shoulders for someone of his heritage. Still, Fynn couldn't help thinking how good it looked on him. When he caught himself, Fynn frowned. "That guy is wound too tight." He reached for his towel and dragged his against his neck.

"He has a right to be." Carson's tone was serious. "After all the crap he's been through in the last few months—he's handling it better than I ever would."

"What kind of things?"

"He lost everything, his family, his career all because he told them he is gay."

"Damn."

"You didn't hear it from me, got it?"

Fynn frowned. "Do I look stupid to you?

Anyway, he's your friend."

"Yeah."

"You know," Fynn said like an afterthought. "There are so many things I could have said to that crack about me doing things to his body."

Carson shook his head but couldn't seem to hide the big smile on his lips. "He didn't say you. He said Attila the Hun."

"And who do you think that referred to?"

"Fair enough." Carson grinned. "See something you like, Attila?"

"What?" Fynn pursed his lips then pushed air through them. "No."

"Me thinks thou protest too much."

"Me thinks thou art an ass." Fynn countered.

"Touché." Carson laughed. "But seriously, though. He's looking to get his career back but it won't be easy. He'll basically have to start from the bottom again and it's killing him."

Fynn said nothing for a second.

"What kind of career?" Fynn asked.

"What?"

"You said he lost his career. What kind of career was it?"

"He's a singer and a dancer," Carson explained, hunching down to fuss with his shoe. "He was huge in Korea. He used to write his own music for a while too. Had to stop though because his songs kept getting censored over there."

"Censored? Why?"

"Well, they were a bit—um—how do you say...they were the kinds that made women and some men drop their drawers and throw them at the stage."

"I see."

"They told him if he wants to keep making music, they'd have to write his songs. That was the beginning of the end. Though his career skyrocketed after that, he wasn't truly happy."

Fynn rolled his shoulders one way then the next. "Well, you have a studio—give him some space."

"It's not that easy. The Korean music industry is a lot more complicated than that."

"How so?"

"There are steps to a singer hitting the scene," Carson explained.

"But I thought you said he was huge in the Kpop world? He shouldn't have to go through any of those steps."

"In a perfect, less judgmental world,, you'd be right." Carson exhaled before focusing his full attention on Fynn. "Even though he was already here and selling like crazy, he can't just release a song and bam! Back. And to make it worse, Jun Tae wants to come back as a whole new artist—new name, new look, definitely a new sound. He's going to have to do some gigs, then a debut stage, a few more gigs, then stop for a few months to gauge the public's reaction to this music, get feedback, make changes then do a comeback stage…"

Fynn rubbed his temples. "You're right. All that is starting to give me a headache."

"Why do you think some Korean boy bands stay together for fifteen twenty years?" Carson asked. "They know precisely what to do, how they're marketed—their people know their demographic extremely well. It's so complicated. Sometimes they form a band when the boys are like…twelve, thirteen but the band doesn't actually debut until they are all eighteen nineteen. There's plenty of work and it takes time."

"Jun Tae doesn't have that much time. How old is he, twenty five? Twenty six?"

"Twenty six."

"There are only a few more years that he's going to look as good as he does now. If he's going to do this, he might want to get on it."

The two began walking from the private space. Before Fynn could say anything else they were in the change room and Jun Tae was pulling his shirt on. He hadn't been swift enough because Fynn saw the tail end of some ink against Jun Tae's right shoulder. Though he said nothing, he couldn't help wondering what the tattoo was of. Jun Tae sat on the bench to haul on his shoes while Carson left them alone to shower.

It took Fynn a little time to gather his stuff. Afterward, he held his towel in one hand, body wash in the other and leaned his back against the lockers. Jun Tae's face was flushed. "You all right?"

"Fine," Jun Tae said, lifting his head. "Just a little sore but that should go away."

"Look, I'm sorry for pushing you so hard today," Fynn said. "I should've warned you."

"I'm not worried about it." Jun Tae said. "Tomorrow, it will hurt and then my body will heal until it'll be like it never happened."

Fynn didn't reply. He pressed his lips into a thin line and hurried back to the stalls. He began running behind the second he stopped to speak with Jun Tae but he just couldn't help it. There was just something in the man's eyes that caught his attention. Making a mental note to press Carson for information later, he turned on the faucet.

"I want to have a party for Jun Tae on Saturday at my place," Carson said, leaning his shoulder against the wall. "Can you come?"

"I have a dance thing in the morning—what time were you thinking?"

"About five-ish? I figured we could throw some meat on the BBQ and then have a few beers. He doesn't like people making a big deal over him."

"So why are you throwing him a party?"

"He won't know it's for him until he gets there." Carson grinned.

"And you think that's a good idea?"

Carson shrugged and headed back toward the lockers.

Fynn sighed and shook his head. "Don't

leave without grabbing the food ma sent for you!"

"Trust me," Carson hollered in reply. "I've been looking forward to tasting those meatballs all night. I won't forget."

Long after he'd left Carson and Jun Tae, Fynn managed to get through the day but he couldn't stop thinking about Jun Tae. The strict purse of his lips, the deep brown of his eyes, bleach blond of his hair—everything about the Korean was so damn attractive. But he wasn't looking for love—right?

Fynn groaned and lifted his face to the water. He didn't even know if Jun Tae was gay.

Only one way to find out!

"Shut up, brain. I mean it."

Battling with his mind, he finished teaching for the night and headed home with a pile of short stories to read and grade. There was the fine print, the part that got him. He hated grading other people's work—he didn't even read reviews before buying a book or seeing a movie. But here he was, sitting in his office, a stack higher than his head. He glared at it a little, then some more then more until the phone rang.

"Yeah, hello?"

"Trix, Carson here."

"Hey, what's up?"

"You wanna go out tonight?" Carson asked. "I managed to score Jun Tae a performance in Korea town and we don't know if anyone will come so it would be nice to…"

"Tell me the time and the place."

"Running from grading stories again?"

Fynn groaned. "Just gimme the address?"

"Fine, be that way." Carson gave another hearty laugh before giving Fynn what he needed. "See you soon."

Fynn hung up before Carson could dig anymore into his psyche. After a quick shower, he got dressed while picking at some leftovers from his mother's place. By the time he was fully dressed, the rest of his food had gone cold so he carried it to the kitchen, left it on the counter and grabbed his cell and keys.

It took a little time to get to the subway. It seemed traffic at nights had become just as bad as the mornings. Still, he found a nice spot close to the entrance, parked and dipped into the station. After using the bank machine, he bought some gum for the change before bypassing the crowded escalator for the stairs. He paid his fare and rushed down another set of steps and ducked into the train just as the doors were closing.

One station phased out followed by another

and soon he was at Bathurst Station. It'd been a while since he visited Korea Town. There wasn't really a need to go. The last time he was there, he'd bought so much tea, he still had some left at home. Scrolling through his phone for the note with the address, he walked south along Bathurst Street then West on Bloor, past Honest Ed's and Snakes and Latte's. He thought of how clever that name was before jay walking across the street to the address Carson had given him.

The moment he paid his entrance fee and stepped inside, he was bombarded by the sound of a mic check. Different conversations around the room turned the air into a loud hum. It took him a few seconds for his eyes to get used to the lighting but soon he caught sight of Carson. He headed in that direction but kept getting stopped by people who recognized him from one show or another.

"You performing tonight?" One asked.

"No. Just here to support a friend," Fynn replied. It wasn't exactly a lie—Jun Tae was a friend of a friend's so technically, he was Fynn's friend. He shrugged unnecessarily and kept moving. Someone else stopped Fynn to ask him the same question and he returned with the same answer then the same rationalization inside his head. Finally, he reached Carson and the two hugged. "I didn't think so many people would recognize me here."

Carson shrugged. "You know how small the music scene is, brother. Korean or black, they know you. Talent is talent."

"Where's Jun Tae?"

"Freaking out in the back," Carson said. "I'm beginning to think this was a bad idea. I mean, he just got here. To kind of just toss him into the deep end like this could scar him for life."

"You're being a drama king. Let me talk to him."

Carson nodded and led the way down a hall into a wide open room. Jun Tae was seated in a corner so still, Fynn had missed him.

"JT?"

"Yeah?" Jun Tae replied without looking up from his hands.

Fynn took a closer look and realized the man was shaking. "There's nothing to be scared about."

"Carson, really?" Jun Tae looked up then. "You invited him?"

"Well, of course I did! And he's right. You don't have to be so nervous."

Jun Tae rose and began pacing.

"Carson, give us a second, alone?" Fynn

asked.

Carson exhaled, nodded and left the room. Fynn caught Jun Tae's hand and pulled. Jun Tae crashed into his chest. Jun Tae moaned but Fynn merely gripped his hips and navigated Jun Tae to his seat. "I could tell you something like *imagine everyone in their underwear*." Fynn said. "But that never works. But here's what I will say. Believe in your talent. If you don't, the crowd will sense it. If you can't do that then don't go out there. Can you do that?"

Jun Tae nodded.

"Don't nod. Say it." Fynn said. "Your talent is like your lover. She wants to hear you tell her she's doing a good job."

"He."

Fynn blinked. "What?"

"He. My lover would be a he."

Fynn chuckled. "Sorry. He. So say it. Say *I*

believe."

Jun Tae seemed hesitant but after Fynn shook his shoulder, Jun Tae tilted his neck from side to side. "I believe."

"I like you mean it."

"I believe," Jun Tae said in a stronger voice.

"Good. Now go out there and show them what you're workin' with."

Chapter Four

For the first time in what felt like forever, Jun Tae took the stage. For the first time ever, he took it not as JT Min but as Jun Tae. The concept of being anyone, anything other than JT Min became so foreign to him, he heaved slightly as though to throw up. Inhaling, he tapped his fingers lightly against his thighs, listening to his name roll off the announcer's tongue and out in the air, impossible to be taken back.

When he was introduced, he could hear

the hushed silence that dawned over the dimly lit club. The attendees drew closer to the stage all at once as if they shared a mind. They knew who he was even if he was using his real name and not some variation of it. The jitters he had surging through him before all came back and for a moment he was frozen. His tongue was stuck to the roof of his mouth and he couldn't seem to remember how to swallow.

He caught sight of Carson, front row center. Carson nodded and a little of the uneasiness passed. Jun Tae shifted and that action pulled his gaze from Carson and forced it to land on Fynn.

Say I believe.

Jun Tae exhaled out his mouth and whispered the one line over and over in his head like something that had gone way past repetition and was fused into the ever present form of a mantra.

I believe.

The music to Rihanna's *Kiss It Better* began and as he kept his focus on Fynn, Jun Tae began seeing the problem with that song. Even as his voice floated over the words, he used Fynn as the one constant, the *thing* that kept him from dropping the mic and running off the stage, the one beauty that kept his voice from cracking. He added impromptu movements to the song, and the crowd went from silence to waving, to whistling to cheering. When he finished, the room erupted in applause and whistles. Jun Tae smiled and bowed. "Thank you," he said. "Thank you."

When he left the stage, the noise continued. Feeling high, as if he'd taken some kind of a drug, he exited the back and was met at the door by Carson and Fynn.

"Whoa, brother!" Carson hugged him tightly, lifted him off the ground and spun him around. "Who knew those hips could move like that?"

Jun Tae flushed but couldn't help laughing. "Aww, come on," Jun Tae said. "Put me down, would you?"

"He gets overly excited from time to time," Fynn said, his voice husky. "You did good. I told you, you would."

"Thanks," Jun Tae said once Carson placed him back on his feet. "I say we celebrate!"

"It was just a performance, Carson," Jun Tae told him. "Not that big of a deal."

"Not that big of a—" Carson looked as if his head would explode. He glanced hurriedly from Jun Tae to Fynn back to Jun Tae. "Brother, did you see what you just did? You had them screaming for more! And he says it's not a big deal!" Carson walked off muttering to himself but because of the din of noise, Jun Tae didn't hear.

"Well, you did it," Fynn said. "How does it feel?"

"Like my first kiss," Jun Tae said without thinking.

When Fynn smirked at him, Jun Tae wanted the ground to open up and swallow him. "Jesus, what the hell was I thinking saying that?"

Fynn laughed. "Don't worry about it. I get what you mean. Come, let me buy you a drink to celebrate."

"You don't have to do that."

"No. But I want to."

Jun Tae took that quiet moment alone with Fynn. And though once they went to the bar they couldn't have a conversation, he pretended they were alone, sitting side by side, sipping on their beers. It was the best time Jun Tae ever spent with a man—he had to admit that.

Eventually, Carson found them with another friend he knew from *back in the day* as he put it. Jun Tae forgot the man's name the second Carson said it but shook the newcomer's hand once and released it. They chitchatted as much as the crowd, music and writhing bodies around them would allow before the new guy excused himself and was swallowed up by the crowd around them.

When Jun Tae was focused again, he saw that Carson was frowning at his cell. "Guys, listen, I have to go."

"Go?" Fynn asked.

"Where?" Jun Tae added.

"Mom has a flat on the 401 and instead of calling AAA like I told her to she wants me to come help her."

"Why does she have AAA if she's not going to use it?" Fynn wanted to know.

Carson shrugged. "Can you take JT home?"

"Yeah, yeah. Go."

"Don't worry about me," Jun Tae assured him. "Help your mom."

Carson looked dejected but he hugged Jun Tae then Fynn before weaving his way through the crowd. Jun Tae inhaled but didn't get much peace for people kept passing by and congratulating him, patting him on the shoulder, shouting above the music to tell him how sexy that was. A few guys even winked at him. For some reason their open flirtations felt strange and almost out of place for Jun Tae had never had that before. He managed a small smile before tapping Fynn on the shoulder.

"You wanna go?" Jun Tae asked. "I'm beginning to feel like a mice in a pit of snakes."

Fynn laughed, paid their tabs and the two exited the club together. Back outside, the temperature had fallen. Jun Tae hadn't been prepared for that. Still he walked, fingers shoved into his pocket beside Fynn back to the subway. When they were seated on the train, he stretched his legs out before him and sighed.

"You won't believe how good that felt," Jun Tae said. "I don't think I could ever explain it."

"I think I could guess," Fynn said. "Like the best thing you ever put in your mouth."

Jun Tae's mind instantly fell into the gutter. "Something like that."

"Carson told me you were a singer in

Korea—boy band?"

"For a while. Then the band fell apart after the other two went for their military service and decided to stay in. I went solo."

"What happened?"

"My sexuality took it all away." Jun Tae couldn't believe his honesty to Fynn. "A long and horrible story I never want to rehash."

"I'm sorry."

"And that's why."

"Why what?" Fynn asked.

"Why I don't want to rehash it." Jun Tae drew his legs in to allow a woman to walk by with a baby stroller to empty seats on the other side. "When I do talk about it, people get this look in their eyes like *you poor baby*. Right before they say *I'm sorry*. No, I'm sorry is for those people who lost something or someone they love. I didn't *lose* anything. It was taken from me."

"I didn't mean anything by it," Fynn explained. "Sometimes we get dealt a bad hand and our world explodes. You're not the only one who goes through shit. What you have to do now is stand up. Cowering in a corner isn't going to help."

"You don't even know me!" Jun Tae muttered like an irritable child. "And I don't cower."

"Uh-huh."

"Truth is." Jun Tae shifted in the side so his back was to everyone else and he could face Fynn. "I feel broken. Like I'm unworthy of anything good. There's this overwhelming sense of loss that fills every part…Do you know what I mean?"

Fynn nodded. "When I was fifteen, my grandfather died. My father and I are close but with Pap Pap—he was my everything. After he was gone, I felt like my world would never be right again. Like it was constantly raining and no matter how hard I tried, it would never stop, like everything I ever was and will ever be was gone the moment he stopped breathing."

"Yeah." Jun Tae flopped back into the seat. "That's precisely how I'm feeling."

"It will get better, as corny as that sounds. I learned that loss is a part of life and we can either go with it or get over it."

"As harsh as that sounds." Jun Tae muttered.

"As harsh as that sounds, yes."

"Next station, Kennedy. Kennedy Station."

Jun Tae looked out the window to see they were just leaving Warden Station, one of the three or four above ground stations in the

Toronto Transit Commission's subway line between Yonge Station and Kennedy. He remembered that from his time there.

"So, have you decided what you'll do about your music?" Fynn asked. "You're good."

"I don't know. I'm indecisive. One minute I'm sure I'm finished with the music industry…"

"*Arriving at Kennedy. Kennedy Station. Doors will open on—the—right.*"

Jun Tae stood. "The next minute, like tonight and especially with the crowd's reaction, I'm back straddling the fence between screw it and let's do this."

"Well, maybe that's because you don't have the right incentive to carry on your music," Fynn said.

The doors chimed and sprang open. The two walked side by side out and then onto the long escalator upward.

"What kind of incentive?" Jun Tae asked.

"I don't know. You'd have to talk to Carson. He's the ideas man."

Jun Tae smiled. But in his head, his incentive had something to do with Fynn Gibbs, a bowl of melted caramel and large, sweet strawberries.

♥

Fynn dropped Jun Tae off at the hotel with a bumped fist. He watched Jun Tae enter the building and after a few more breaths, he climbed back into his car and headed home. All the way there he wondered if he'd be able to pick himself up the way Jun Tae wanted. The answer wasn't immediate and his mind switched gears to the pain he saw in the Korean man's eyes each time they talked about Jun Tae's life. There was something so hard about watching a man that broken struggle to his feet again.

Even as he parked and entered his house through the back door, his mind was still on Jun Tae. By the time he locked up, set the alarm and stripped for the shower, he was now focused on the way Jun Tae's body moved to the beats of *Kiss it Better*. He didn't know any Asian boys who could whine like that and it drove him crazy. Fynn lifted his face to the downpour of water as fragments of rap lyrics swirled through his mind mingled with glimpses of Jun Tae's thrusting hips.

He had to cut his shower short, wrap a towel around his hips and darted for his notepad and pen. Fynn scribbled until he had two complete rap verses before climbing into bed.

His body was tired but his mind kept going until almost six in the morning. He managed to get a couple of hours to sleep then he was up, hauling on his clothes and darting for the door.

At Jun Tae's hotel, he found what room the man was in and rushed into the elevator. The ride up was relatively short to a normal person but Fynn tapped his foot impatiently. He could barely wait for the door to open before he quickly read the number sequence and made his way to Jun Tae's door. Fynn knocked and waited, impatiently tapping his foot on the carpeted floor.

Jun Tae opened the door shirtless with a mug in his hand. His brow shot upward when he saw Fynn.

"Fynn? What're you doing here?"

"Can I come in?" Fynn asked.

"Um—sure." Jun Tae stepped aside.

"Remember last night we were talking about incentives?" Fynn asked.

"Yeah."

"Well, I got one for you."

In the kitchenette area, Jun Tae set his mug down and leveled his brown stare onto Fynn. "Okay?"

Fynn took that moment to pull the page he'd torn out of his notebook and unfolded it. He laid it flat on the counter. "Read this."

Jun Tae picked it up and Fynn paced the space.

"Is this yours?" Jun Tae asked.

"Yeah. I couldn't get it out of my head," Fynn told him. "I figure if you could write a hook and verses around that, and I can talk Carson into some space at the studio, we'd have something to put out in the world—if you want to work with me that is."

Jun Tae chuckled. "It's really good man. I don't know if I got it in me to write something around this—I feel almost like I'd be letting you down."

"Cut that shit out, would you?" Fynn frowned and faced him. "Don't think about all that bull. Carson said your stuff used to get censored or banned in Korea, right? So you have it in you to build a song with this. It should be sexy, hot, but still classy, you know?"

"I wouldn't know where to begin. You know how they say once you learn to ride a bike you never forget?"

"Yeah?"

"They're full of shit." Jun Tae took a breath. "I feel like I did forget and besides, I have nothing to draw from."

Fynn frowned and charged across the space.

He cradled Jun Tae's face in his palms and slammed his mouth over his, shoving his tongue forward demanding to be admitted. Jun Tae moaned under his assault and clutch the back of Fynn's shirt even as their tongue swirled around each other's. Fynn trembled and pulled back.

Jun Tae's eyes remained closed.

"How about now?" Fynn asked, his voice surprisingly raspy to his own ears.

"I think I could come up with something," Jun Tae whispered.

"Good." Fynn released him and pulled out one of his business cards. He set it on the counter. "My cell is on the back. Call me when you got something."

Jun Tae opened his eyes but didn't speak. Instead he nodded. Fynn took that moment to all but run from the hotel suite. When he was finally in the safety of his car, he covered his face as he tried slowing his heart down. Instead, Fynn's shoulders rose and fell dramatically as his body overheated. He wasn't sure what came over him—perhaps it was anger at Jun Tae doubting himself or just residual emotions from the night before. Whatever it was, Fynn prayed it wouldn't come over him again. He'd crossed the line with Jun Tae and after Jun Tae writes the song, Fynn would apologies—not for the kiss, but for the way it'd happened.

Yet, Fynn wanted it to happen again.

"Damn it." He muttered. "Damn! Damn! Shit!"

He wound up at his father's office but Denny was in a meeting. Though he could talk to his mother, he just knew she'd spend the whole time gushing over how he was *growing up* and how she was *happy he was dating* even though it was only a kiss. Fynn waited, standing by the glass of his father's office atop the world, looking down like a brooding superhero watching over his city.

The sun was barely up, and already when he turned his eyes toward the 401, it was backed up for as far as he could see.

"Son!" Denny said. "I didn't know you were coming."

"Sorry to just drop in." Fynn turned and hugged his father. "But I wanted to talk to you about something that I really shouldn't be putting this much thought into but I can't help it."

Denny dropped a file on his desk and exhaled long and loud. "Okay. Talk to me."

"Um—I kissed someone."

"O-kay." Denny dragged out. "You have kissed people before—men and women—and your mother and I did talk to you about the straight and gay birds and bees. So what am I missing?"

Fynn made a face. "I couldn't control myself! That's what you're missing." He fell into one of his father's chairs. "And he's going through hell right now. I had no right dropping that on him."

"Who?"

"Jun Tae."

Denny arched a brow. "Jun-Who-Now?"

"Carson's friend from Korea." Fynn added. "He's just so—he has no self esteem left. None. His parents and all the other shady people in his life sucked him dry of everything."

"Well, is he gay?"

"Yes."

"So I'm lost, what's the problem?"

"I gave him no warning," Fynn told his

father. "None. I just plopped one on him, assuming he'd want that."

"Did he kiss you back?" Denny asked.

"Well, yeah."

Denny laughed. "Good. So you won't need a lawyer."

"Dad. Seriously."

"Look, son, life is complicated enough. If this Jun Tae guy didn't want you to kiss him he wouldn't have kissed you back. Trust me."

"I have to apologize."

"Oh no!" Denny said, waving a hand. "That's the absolute wrong thing to do."

"But!"

"Trix, listen. I'm not gay so I wouldn't know everything. But if you kiss someone, they return it and you say you're sorry it wreaks havoc on their self-esteem. It makes it seem as if you kissing them was an accident, one you regret."

"But I don't regret the kiss, just how it happened."

"It won't matter." Denny sighed. "That conversation would be like—like—your mother asking me if a pants make her butt look big. There's no winning that one. Believe me."

Fynn arched a brow at Denny.

"Don't worry so much about it," Denny continued. "I'm pretty sure the next time you see him he would have forgotten."

Fynn exhaled.

"You want to come back later and have lunch with an old man?"

Fynn laughed. "Sure, old man. What time?"

"About one?" Denny grinned.

"I'll be here."

Chapter Five

The next couple of days, Jun Tae spent it in a rented car driving around the city. He stopped at a local real estate office and hired a realtor to find him a condo. With that underway, he went shopping for some clothes, notebooks and pens, markers and highlighters and a few other things he would need to write. He even purchased a new tablet and iPod for his music and a gift card so he could buy music. He'd left everything in Korea when he ran.

Ideas to add to the rap Fynn left him kept bubbling inside his head. After a while, he could barely contain the excitement. The kiss he'd shared with Fynn mingled with his racing heart and the arousal he felt sent the lyrics and melody tumbling from him and onto the page once he finally got a chance to sit down and write. But he sat on the song for those few days. Jun Tae didn't even tell Carson even though he and his friend met up for dinner a few times.

At the end of the week his realtor called him to see a condo that just went on the market. The seller was trying to get rid of it fast because he scored his dream job in Dubai. After taking a look at it with Carson, Jun Tae put in an offer and the two went out for ice-cream while Jun Tae waited to hear back from his agent.

"So, I have to head into Japan for a few days," Carson said.

"On business?"

"Yeah. There's a singer everyone's gushing about in the underground and I want to go take a listen."

"Nice. Good luck."

Carson nodded. "You going to be okay here by yourself?"

"Of course."

"Even so, I'm gonna have Fynn keep an eye on you—not like that, you know? Just make sure if you need a friend or something."

"I'll be okay until you get back." Jun Tae assured him. "But just in case I needed to find him…"

Carson laughed and pulled out his wallet. He dug around in it until he found a business card then got his pen. He wrote on the back of it and handed the card to Jun Tae. "The studio space he uses for his dancing is on the back. His house is on the back as well."

"I'm not going to his house. That would be kind of weird."

"Depends on the reason you want to see him and how freaky you like it."

Jun Tae groaned. "Would you cut it out? He and I are not going to be anything but friends. I don't even know if he likes me."

"Don't be a dope." Carson shoved what was left of his cone into his mouth and chewed. "Fynn isn't a talker—well not a big talker I should say, but he wouldn't have taken the time to encourage you the way he had if he didn't see something he liked."

"He encouraged me alright."

"What does that mean?"

"What does what mean?" Jun Tae couldn't keep eye contact.

"That crack about the encouragement."

"What're you, a lawyer?" Jun Tae asked. "Why do you have to question everything? I just made a comment."

Carson tilted his head in that way that said *don't piss on my head and tell me it's raining.* "Seriously, JT?"

Jun Tae took a breath. "He kissed me."

"What?"

"I liked it."

Carson laughed. "There you go, brother. He likes you."

"I'm not dumb enough to believe that." Jun Tae chuckled. "He did it because he thought it would turn me on enough to make me write lyrics."

"And did it?"

"Did it what?"

"I'm talking to a brick wall." Carson groaned. "Turn you on! Aren't you paying attention?"

Jun Tae tried walking away without answering the question but Carson merely ran after him then began walking backward before him.

"You're not getting away without answering this," Carson said. "Did kissing Fynn Gibbs give you a boner?"

"Could we not talk about what gives me boners? Please?" Jun Tae knew his face was red. He could feel the heat rise from his toes then pooled against his cheeks and forehead.

"Ah-ha!" Carson laughed and pointed. "You can't lie to me, brother. Your eyes tell me everything."

"You know, some straight men wouldn't want to know that."

"What can I say?" Carson shrugged. "I'm very curious by nature."

"He's good looking, okay?"

"But?"

"Who says there's a but?" Jun Tae

shrugged. "There is no but."

"Oh, yes there is." Carson rolled his eyes. "I know you very well, JT. And when you say things like that, there's always a but. You felt the fire when he kissed you. The raging, passionate *fire!*"

"You're an ass, you know that?"

"But an ass you adore, brother." Carson laughed out loud. "Listen, there's no need to be shy. I'm a straight man but even I can admit that Fynn is a good looking chap. If you felt something from his kiss, man up and go after him. Don't let someone else come in and take your man."

"He's not mine to begin with." Jun Tae frowned.

"That's your fault at this point." Carson walked off ahead of him just as Jun Tae's phone rang.

He answered it and it was the agent telling him he got the place. All he needed to do was bring a check and head down to the office to sign some papers. After thanking the woman, he jogged after Carson.

"You got the place." Carson stopped to face him.

"Yep."

"Well, now you have some roots in the ground." Carson grinned. "Like it or not, brother, you're stayin'."

"I guess I am." They walked silently, side by side until they reached the shores of lake Ontario. They sat in the sand, staring out over the water. "What kind of men does he like?"

"Who?"

"Fynn."

Carson sighed. "That's kind of a hard question to answer. Fynn doesn't really date,

date. He's been out with a couple of guys but he didn't like either of them and one ended in a disaster."

"Just a couple?"

"Yeah. He's searching for forever, two point five kids, white picket fence with a hotrod in the garage, that sort of thing. The men around here just want to hit it and quit it. That's not Fynn's style."

Jun Tae's heart soared. "Mine either."

"Well, maybe the two of you can be boring together."

"He kissed me, remember? Nothing sleep inducing about that."

Carson laughed. "I'll take your word for it, brother. Just know, if you do decide to seduce Fynn Gibbs, I suggest show him your heart, the way you feel about your music, your craft, then give him chocolate."

Jun Tae laughed. "Chocolate, eh?"

The wind ruffled his hair and he looked out at the water to see a lone sailboat making its way over the waves. There was something peaceful about staring at the water. A calm Jun Tae had never experienced before swam over him. It caused him to breath deeper, to enjoy the cool breeze and warm sun a little more.

"How long are you going to be in Japan?"

"About a week," Carson replied. "Give or take a few days."

"It's going to suck not having you here. I don't have any other friends in the city, you know?"

"That's not entirely true, is it? You have two friends in the city."

"Who?"

"Fynn."

Jun Tae chuckled. "We'll see."

♥

Fynn hefted the large pot with water onto the stove. Whenever his mother made soup she went all out. The only thing was she usually went over board and make too much. This time, she was using the medium size pot. He said nothing out loud to her about it but merely turned on the stove beneath it, added some salt like she always told him to do along with thyme and scallion.

When she finally entered, he was sitting at the island, peering at lyrics that Jun Tae had sent him. They were sexy—not vulgar sexy—but the kind that would bring a grown man to his knees. He knew Jun Tae was talented, from what Carson said, but this was beyond anything he'd expected. Then he remembered Jun Tae wrote it after Fynn had kissed him.

Would it be egotistic to think Fynn did something to Jun Tae, something primal that turned him on?

That's what you wanted, right, so what gives?

Fynn rubbed the back of his neck.

"What's wrong?" Paulette asked.

Fynn glanced up from his paper to see her kneading dumplings in a large bowl. He watched the way her strong fingers gripped the dough and massaged it to the shape she wanted. "Nothing is wrong—it's just—I kissed Carson's friend the other day."

"Your father told me."

Fynn groaned. "Of course he did."

"What? He's my *baby* and you're my baby so…we share."

"Sure." Fynn smiled. "Anyway, then I told

him to write with the inspiration from that kiss—more or less."

"And?"

Fynn turned the paper so she could read it without stopping what she'd been doing. When she was finished, Paulette shook her head with a smile. "How old did you say this cat was?"

"My age."

"That's some Barry White meets Marvin Gay vibe right there," Paulette said, dancing around the kitchen with a dumpling hoisted above her head. "He's good."

"I know."

"All that from one kiss, huh?"

"Don't read too much into it, Ma." He took the dumpling from her and set it on the plate just as she wrapped her arms around his hips and pulled him into the waltz. "Seriously, Ma!"

Paulette laughed. "Oh you're no fun. Look,

if he wrote that song after locking lips with you, there's something there."

"And how do I know for sure."

"You don't. But the bible says *seek and ye shall find.* So, go forth and seek!"

Fynn rubbed his eyes. When she started talking like women from days of old, all he wanted to do was bang his forehead into the counter. "Ma, it's not that simple."

"Sure it is. Your father and I wouldn't have met if he didn't come looking for me." She set the dumplings aside to peel yams. "We met briefly at a bookstore on College Street called *She Says Boom*. I told him my name—that time I was working at that night at a club on Richmond. It was more of a *come get me* type deal. If he didn't show up my life would have moved on. But, he did. He came seeking."

"I understand." Fynn filled a bowl with

water, added a half cup of vinegar to it then mixed unnecessarily with his index finger. "But this is a bit different."

"Why?" She plopped some peeled yams into the vinegar water. "Because you're gay? Love is love, Trix—gay or straight. It generally works the same way. If it's mean to be, nothing will stop it."

"Whoa! Who said anything about love?"

"No one. But I'm an old woman, Trix. I don't have the patient for beating around the bush. The only reason this kiss is bothering you so much and could influence him to write that song is if there is something more there."

"Ma…"

"All I'm saying." Paulette picked up another yam. "Don't close a door you don't have to."

He stared at her for a bit then picked up

knife. He gently peeled some potatoes and chocho for her and placed them on a plate to the side. Once he was finished, he washed his hands and took a seat over the lyrics again. With his mother's words still floating around in his head, he knew he had to work on the song with Jun Tae. If not to make a hit, but to see just how much chemistry the two of them could ignite.

While his mom cooked, he excused himself to the front yard. He dialed the hotel, asked for Jun Tae's room and waited. When Jun Tae's voice finally came over the line, Fynn tumbled to the top step of the porch and licked his lips. "Hey—I read the lyrics you sent."

"And?"

"I really like them. Wanna try recording it?"

Jun Tae laughed. "Of course. But we have

to wait until Carson gets back."

"Nope. He has a few free spaces. He gave them to us if you want, that is."

"Tell me when and where and I'll be there."

Fynn's heart raced. "How about tonight? I'll pick you up?"

"Is this a date, Fynn?"

Fynn's breath caught in his throat. He smiled. "It depends."

"On?"

"What you're wearing tonight."

Jun Tae coughed.

Fynn couldn't help laughing out loud. "You all right?"

"I-I'm fine."

"Good. The session starts at eight because another band is in ahead of us. So pick you up at seven?"

"I'll be ready."

Chapter Six

Jun Tae paced the hotel suite, periodically staring at the clock. Each time he looked, it was closer to seven when Fynn was supposed to pick him up. The nerves he was experiencing was worse than anything he'd ever had happen to him. Things were a little heated for him when Fynn was around but after the kiss, Jun Tae wasn't sure how he'd be able to face Fynn.

At about five minutes to seven, the sound he'd been waiting for came. Jun Tae almost jumped a foot into the air. Frowning, he smoothed his hands over the black dress shirt he wore then down along his jean clad thighs. It took everything in him not to rush to the door and fling it open. Slowly, Jun Tae made his way to the door as another knock came. Finally he was face to face with Fynn Gibbs and Jun Tae wanted another kiss.

"Hey, ready?" Fynn asked, leaning his shoulder into the doorframe.

"Um—almost. You're early."

"Not by much."

"Come in." Jun Tae stepped aside. "I need to find socks."

Fynn walked by him and the moment caused Jun Tae to get a strong whiff of Fynn's cologne. Jun Tae knew if he didn't hurry up so they could get out of the privacy of the hotel room, they would never leave. Quickly, he found a pair of socks that didn't even match what he was wearing but Jun Tae didn't care. He hauled them on as quickly as he could, checked to make sure he had some cash and his credit card.

After a few seconds of trying to find the bag he'd packed to take with them, Jun Tae followed Fynn out of the hotel and into Fynn's car. It was nice, black leather seat with coffee-coloured trims and a state of the art stereo system. It occurred to him that Carson hadn't really told him much about Fynn, like what he did for a living. The car they were in plus all the obvious additions and alterations must be at least—Jun Tae looked around the interior of the car—three hundred grand. Not wanting to be rude, Jun Tae turned his attention outside rather than ask how much precisely did the vehicle cost.

"Sheesh," Jun Tae mused. "Toronto sure

has changed since the last time I was here."

"When was the last time you were here?"

"Two years ago."

"We measure progress in cat years."

Jun Tae grinned at that. It was the first time he'd heard that but he quite liked it. "I guess. Has Carson called you since leaving?"

"No. But it's not unusual for him not to when he's in meetings," Fynn said. The turn signal clicked as he switched lanes. "He has to talk this guy into signing with him. I'm pretty sure that will take a little time."

"I guess."

"You okay?"

Jun Tae nodded. "Hey, Porter Street is coming up, right?"

"Yeah. Why?"

"There used to be an ice-cream shop there that's opened all night—is it still there?"

Fynn laughed. "It's still there but we can't stop now. We will when we're finished and heading home, okay?"

"Home. Yeah."

They turned into a parking lot with a sign that announced they were entering private property and that unauthorized vehicles would be tagged and or towed at owner's expense. Jun Tae stared at the sign until he could no longer see the wording due to the darkness. When he turned again, it was in time to see that Fynn had pulled up to a gate and was leaning precariously out the window to tap against a security pad. Soon, it beeped and the large gate clicked and began slowly pulling open.

"Where are we going?" Jun Tae asked.

"Carson always makes me park back here," Fynn explained, pulling himself back in. "It's his private parking spaces."

"Nice."

Fynn drove in and parked right outside a silver door. Jun Tae climbed from the vehicle, stretched his back and reached into the back seat for his bag. They entered the studio to find a man sitting behind the board, playing around with some beats. Jun Tae frowned as Fynn bumped fist with the stranger then hugged him.

"Jun Tae, this is Maxim Roscov," Fynn said. "Max, this is Jun Tae Min."

Jun Tae shook the man's hand but not because he wanted to. He set his bag down, removed his jacket and waited. Fynn and Maxim had a short conversation before Fynn led Jun Tae into the recording room. "I thought we were going to be alone."

"You did?" Fynn leant his shoulder against the frame and crossed his arms over his impressive chest. "If you wanted to be alone with me, Jun Tae, all you have to do is say so."

"I don't know what you're talking about." Jun Tae pulled his lyrics out and a pen. "Can we do this please?"

"This conversation is not over."

"Oh trust me, Fynn, it *is* over."

"You guys wanna run through it a few times?" Maxim's voice came through the speakers.

"I think we…" Fynn began.

"Yes, please." Jun Tae interrupted. "Can you play some music and let me go?

"Hold on. Let me grab my lyrics."

Jun Tae held his breath until Fynn returned. The two worked together to figure out where the rap verses would sound good and off they went. Jun Tae slipped the headphones on, and stepped to his microphone. He glanced over at Fynn who seemed ready. When the music began playing, Jun Tae set his paper on the stand before him and cleared his throat.

"*Once you press play, don't ask me to stop,*" he sang.

They didn't get through the whole thing before having to stop. Jun Tae just couldn't get the words out. Each time he reached a certain part he had to stop and clear his throat.

"Jun Tae? You okay?"

"I can't do this." Jun Tae's voice was small. "How can I sing about this kind of….and this isn't so that you kiss me again—I'm just saying it doesn't feel right."

Fynn nodded. "I see." Without another word, Fynn moved the microphone above Jun Tae's head so when Jun Tae stepped behind it, he had to face Fynn. "For the next two hours, Jun Tae, I'm your lover."

The air caught in Jun Tae's throat,

choking him. He coughed until his eyes burned and his chest throb. Fynn rubbed his back but Jun Tae stepped away from his touch. "But…" Jun Tae managed.

Fynn shook his head. "No. No buts. Everything you've written in this song, you will be doing to me. Let's pretend for the next two hours you want my body. But before we get to the bedroom, before I give you access to what's under my clothes, you have to convince me that you want it."

"Fynn, I…"

The music started again.

"Go ahead, Jun Tae. Convince me."

Jun Tae lifted his head and met Fynn's eyes. This time when the words left his lips, he couldn't hear them. He felt them, sliding from his lips from the very depths of his heart. Every fibre of his being responded to the song and the deep, heated brown of Fynn's eyes didn't quench the thirst building inside him.

He paused for Fynn to rap his sections and by the time the song ended, Jun Tae couldn't breathe. He staggered away from the microphone and was kept from falling to the ground by a wall behind him.

Fynn approached him, pressed a hand against the wall beside Jun Tae's head. "Maybe you need a cigarette. I need one and I don't even smoke."

"I'm glad you think this is funny." Jun Tae groaned.

"Funny?" Fynn questioned, taking Jun Tae's hand and bringing it to the front of his pants. "How funny do you think that was to me?"

Jun Tae gasped and yanked his hand back. Fynn was hard and throbbing beneath his palm.

"I guess you and I have two very different definitions of what funny means."

♥

After his lectures for the day, Fynn made his way down to the dance studio. It'd been a few days before he got some practice in and with the song he and Jun Tae were working on, he probably should get some routines together. Carson was talking about a video but that wouldn't go on the table to Jun Tae until Carson returned. After a while, he sat on the floor with his back against the wall wondering what he was really nervous about with Jun Tae. Was it the fact Jun Tae was so broken and lacked self confidence? Fynn knew he couldn't bring someone like that to his bed—they'd bore him to tears. And besides, if he did anything to hurt Jun Tae even more, Fynn just knew it would break his heart as well.

Still, he felt something for Jun Tae, a certain pull that excited Fynn. He finished his workout and was about to head home when his cell rang. He tossed his bag into the back seat of his car, pulled behind the wheel and closed the door before answering.

"Fynn?"

"Hey Jun Tae." Fynn was stunned to hear from Jun Tae. But he cleared his throat and shifted in his seat. "How are you?"

"I'm okay." Jun Tae said. "Are you—are you busy tonight?"

"No."

"What were you planning on doing?"

"Try and get some writing done after seeing my parents."

"Um…"

"Jun Tae?"

"Yeah?"

Fynn smiled. "Talk to me. You called me for a reason so don't be nervous."

"Sorry. I'm not used to doing anything like this." Jun Tae cleared his throat. "I had all my stuff moved into the new condo and I just—I need someone to help me kind of celebrate the new place. I don't have anyone else and Carson is in Japan and I know you might have better things to do but I was kind of hoping that—shit, sorry. I shouldn't have called."

"Jun Tae?"

"Yeah?"

"I'd love to."

Silence.

"Jun?"

"I-I'm sorry. Did you say yes?"

Fynn laughed softly. "Yes. I'd love to. So what're we going to do?"

"Oh. Oh wow. I—I mean, I don't know. I didn't think you'd say yes so I didn't make any other plans beyond asking.."

"I see. Why don't I bring over some food, and we can just hang out?"

"Sure. I'll text you the address, okay?"

"Okay. See you tonight."

Jun Tae hung up and even as Fynn did the same and dropped the phone on the passenger seat, he couldn't help smiling. There was no reason to freak out about being alone with Jun Tae. He'd already kissed the guy and lately he couldn't seem to stop flirting with him. Whether or not that led to anything was yet to be seen. Deep down he hoped something came of it, other than their collaboration, that is. Making his way home, he took a shower and dug through his closet for the perfect outfit. By the time he was finished, his clothes was on the floor of the massive walk-in closet. Still, he couldn't seem to decide. Eventually, he settled on a simple, plain black tee, black leather jacket and black jeans. He slid his feet in a pair of black converse sneakers. For jewelry he strung a silver necklace around his neck, with a matching wrist watch.

His first stop after leaving home was at his parents. He didn't tell them he was on his way to see Jun Tae. They'd have more questions than he had answers to.

After kissing his mother and hugging his father, he made another detour for food and a couple bottles of wine and sodas. Fynn then found the address to Jun Tae's new place. He parked outside in the visitor's parking spot and stared up at the luxury condo.

After taking a deep breath, he carried the loot to the front and called Jun Tae.

"Hey, hello?" Jun Tae said.

"Hey, it's Fynn. Can you let me in?"

"Oh, right. In penthouse two."

The door buzzed and clicked. He balanced the food on one arm to pull the door open. The ride up was a little slow but he waited until the elevator stopped on the thirtieth floor. Jun Tae met him there and used his security card to access the penthouse.

"You bought a lot of stuff," Jun Tae said. "You didn't have to do that. I ordered a couple of pizzas that just arrived."

"Look at the bright side, we won't run out of food." Fynn followed him through the open space to the kitchen. He set the goodies on the counter and turned to look around. "This place is beautiful. Didn't you just buy it?"

"Yes. I had to give them a little extra so I could move in so quickly." Jun Tae leaned into the glass wall and crossed his arms. "Money makes the world go round."

"I suppose." Fynn rested his back on the counter. "Can I get the tour?"

"Right. Where do you want to start?"

"Well, we should leave the bedroom for last."

Jun Tae laughed. "Come on."

They toured the condo. It was lovely. There were boxes almost everywhere and Jun Tae had yet to put anything on the walls. Finally they made it to the bedroom. Fynn walked past the bed to the glass walls and looked out. The view of the city and the lake was spectacular. He could see for miles. When he bought his house he'd wanted a condo but couldn't justify the price over a house with a backyard and his swimming pool.

"I brought you a glass of wine." Jun Tae's voice was soft behind him.

Fynn turned to accept the glass and smiled. He lifted it and rolled one shoulder. "To new beginnings."

"I can drink to that," Jun Tae admitted before sipping. "Come, we should eat before everything gets cold."

"Yeah—in a minute." Fynn caught Jun Tae's arm and their eyes met. "What're we doing, really? Can I keep pretending I don't want to kiss you again?"

Jun Tae's beautiful pink lips parted in a soundless gasp. He dragged his tongue over them. "You only kissed me to prove a point," he said. "I get it. There's no reason to do it again."

"So you just want to be friends?"

"I don't know what I want," Jun Tae said. "All I can be sure about is we can never sleep together."

"And why is that?"

Jun Tae pulled his arm away and put some space between them. "I already embarrassed my family enough. Getting into a relationship would only make it worse."

"You can't really believe that."

Jun Tae shrugged and left the room.

It was hard for Fynn to comprehend. He'd been given the brush off before but this was a new one. Rubbing his free hand against the back of his neck, he walked into the kitchen and silently grabbed one of the plates Jun Tae had set out. He searched through the pizza and dished himself out a slice of cheese and a pepperoni slice. He added some rice from one of his boxes and some chicken and stew from another. He sat with Jun Tae at the table and though he ate, his mind was a mile away. His mind was in Korea wondering what kind of parents would make their child feel that indulging in the carnal was something to be embarrassed about.

The thought made things easier for him then.

"We can't keep getting together," Fynn said.

"What? Why not?"

Fynn chewed on a piece of pizza then wiped his mouth. "I can't just be friends with you, Jun Tae. There is no way for me to keep seeing you and not want you."

"What about the song we've already done? I can't perform it alone."

"That I can do with you. On stage we will work the crowd like crazy but…"

Jun Tae took a breath. "I'm sorry I'm not strong enough…I'm sorry."

"Jun Tae, you can't carry your parent's hate on your shoulders," Fynn said. "You aren't meant to live the rest of your life based on what they like or don't like. Your parents don't get it and they aren't trying to get it. Why should you set aside your happiness?"

"It's not that easy."

"Of course it is." Fynn took a drink from his glass and set it back on the table. "I want you, Jun Tae. There. I said it. I think about you more than I've thought of anyone other man and all we shared was a kiss. But me wanting isn't enough. You have to be there with me too and since you're not I have to figure out a way to move on from that."

"I'm sorry."

"Stop saying that." Fynn shook his head.

"There's nothing to be sorry about. This kind of thing happens all the time. Look, let's talk about something else. Have you heard from Carson?"

"Yeah. He called earlier. He said he would call you later today."

"Good." Fynn nodded. "Did he say anything about the track?"

Jun Tae nodded. "He likes it. Said there are a few things he had to iron out but will talk to us about releasing the audio on youtube first then if it has a great reception he'll start circulating it. Even suggested we make a video but won't do that until all three of us had a chance to sit down and talk."

"That's amazing news. This will help your career back on track for sure."

"I don't know if I want that as much as I did before."

"What do you mean? This is your livelihood, a way to make your money. How can you give that up?"

"I'm not. Hell, I'm not remotely good at anything else. What I'm saying is I don't know if I'm as vested into it as I was before."

Fynn sat back in his chair and leveled his gaze on Jun Tae. You're not making much sense."

"I—ah—I've been thinking about what you said about my happiness."

"Oh yeah?" Fynn ripped off a piece of chicken and pushed it into his mouth.

"Yeah."

"And what came of that?"

Jun Tae dropped his paper napkin on the table, pushed his chair back and rose. He walked around the table, knelt beside Fynn and curled his fingers against the back of Fynn's neck. "I'm going to fight for it."

Before Fynn could say a word, Jun Tae pulled him forward. Their lips crashed together like waves into a sandy show. Fynn pulled back to catch is breath only to lean in for more. This time when their mouths meet, he couldn't think and he didn't care. He buried his fingers into Jun Tae's hair, pulled the tie out and gripped the hair tightly in his palm. This kiss would last. This kiss had his everything in it. This kiss was—absolutely everything.

Jun Tae moaned. "Yes," he whispered, reaching up to frame Fynn's face with his palms. "I like this new turn of events much better."

Chapter Seven

Though Jun Tae's heart raced like crazy inside his chest, he took Fynn's hand and led him down the hall to the bedroom. He motioned to the bed and Fynn took a seat. Jun Tae watched as Fynn leaned back on his palms, with his brown gaze burning a hole into Jun Tae's soul. He removed his clothes, slowly but Fynn never stopped staring at him. The moment he was naked, Jun Tae knew there was no turning back. Though Fynn's heated stare made him feel slightly self conscious, he couldn't help how sexy he thought that was.

"Turn around," Fynn said.

Jun Tae did as Fynn wanted and could feel Fynn's eyes caressing, hot, over his skin.

"It's a panther," Fynn said. "The tattoo is of a panther."

"Yes. They used to call my grandfather *Pyobeom.* It means panther in my language."

"Do you regret getting it—especially after falling out with your family?"

Jun Tae shook his head feeling defiant. "No. Fynn, I'm naked, with you in my bedroom and all you want to talk about is my tattoo?"

Fynn laughed softly. "I was merely curious—come to me, Jun Tae."

With a deep breath, Jun Tae turned and made his way across the space before climbing to sit across Fynn's lap. When Fynn's arms went around him, he couldn't help feeling he was precisely where he should be. He was with the one person he should be with and nothing ever made him feel that before.

He leaned Fynn back onto the bed, and allowed Fynn to make love to him. Jun Tae's nerves vanished and he found Fynn's mouth again. In those moments, nothing else mattered. All that he could focus on was the fact that Fynn Gibbs was naked, in his bed and touching him with more tenderness than anyone else. He gasped and arched into Fynn's hands and as much as he tried telling his brain this was just a onetime thing, the love coming through Fynn's fingertips screamed more.

But Jun Tae's undoing was when Fynn became a part of him. When he felt Fynn hard and throbbing within him, Jun Tae knew there was no going back to just being friends. There was no more hiding from Fynn and the carnal insanity Fynn inspired within Jun Tae. He dug his nails into Fynn's arms, wrapped himself around him and when the whole world exploded, he wrapped his arms around Fynn and pulled his mouth to him.

When they flopped to the bed together, Jun Tae couldn't help the tremble that surged through him. His mind was blissfully numb and all he could do was smile.

"Are you okay?" Fynn whispered, leaning in to kiss at Jun Tae's shoulder. "I don't know if I was too…"

"I'm good, I promise." Jun Tae swallowed the lump in his throat. "I just—right now I can't think."

"Is that a good thing or a bad thing?"

"A very good thing." Jun Tae pushed to his elbow and looked down into Fynn's face. "What did we do?"

"We slept together." Fynn replied

simply, a grin spreading his lips. "Please don't tell me you're regretting this already."

"No." Jun Tae replied. "No regrets. I just have to figure out a way of reconcile myself with everything that is happening."

Fynn lifted his body and dropped a kiss on Jun Tae's mouth. "No. Don't do that. We're going to go through his like it's a relationship we want to keep. We're going to be ourselves and grow together. That's what I want."

"But you barely know me."

Fynn smiled. "I know you more intimately than most others. There is time for all that. Right now, let's make music, and love and no pressure."

Jun Tae smiled. "You know one of the reasons I really like you, Fynn Gibbs?"

"What's that?"

"You make things uncomplicated."

"Hey, I'm too young for a stroke." Fynn laughed and wrapped his arms around Jun Tae to pull their bodies together again. "Now, round two."

Jun Tae didn't complain. He enjoyed ever second with Fynn, ever touch, ever softly, whispered word. When they finally settled in for bed, Jun Tae snuggled into Fynn's side. The second he closed his eyes, his phone began ringing. Though he meant to ignore it, Fynn reached for it and handed it to him. With a groan, he answered it.

"Hello?"

Nothing.

"Hello?" Jun Tae repeated.

A faint static noise.

"Hello?"

Dial tone.

He looked down at the face of the phone

and tilted his head. It was a private call. With a mental shrug, he leaned over Fynn to set the phone back on the bedside table.

"No one there?"

"Nope."

"Come here baby." Fynn said, pulling Jun Tae close.

Jun Tae cuddled into Fynn and tossed a possessive arm across Fynn's body. For the first time ever, Jun Tae closed his eyes and slept peacefully in a man's arms without any guilt or shame. When he woke up the next morning, Fynn wasn't beside him. So many thoughts flashed through his mind from Fynn was having second thoughts to Fynn left in the middle of the night. He slowly climbed out of bed, pulled on a pair of track pants that was strung over a nearby chair and made his way out to wander the condo.

For some reason he didn't call out for Fynn. He expected to be alone. His heart thundered inside his chest, drowning everything out. Each step carried him further toward the kitchen where he found Fynn, shirtless in the kitchen cooking.

"You're still here," Jun Tae said.

Fynn glanced around at him before going back to his pot. "Yes. Why wouldn't I be?"

"I don't know."

"Come on, Jun." Fynn turned around and approached him. He rubbed his palms up and down Jun Tae's arms before kissing the side of his head. "You have to trust me."

"I know. I woke up and you weren't there and all these thoughts just filled my head."

"I was going to surprise you," Fynn said between a few other kisses. "Ever had breakfast in bed?"

"No." Jun Tae wrapped his arms around his neck. "It seems I'm doing a lot of firsts with you."

Fynn smirked and Jun Tae's heart soared.

"Why don't you crawl back in bed?" Fynn asked. "I'll bring you some food and—coffee or tea?"

"Tea. Nothing in it."

Fynn nodded. They shared another scorching kiss and Jun Tae turned to leave. Fynn tapped him lightly on the bum as he walked away and Jun Tae glanced back to see Fynn smiling. It felt good to know someone wanted him the way Fynn did. There was no pretense in Fynn's eyes, no hesitation in his touch or the way he spoke to Jun Tae.

He climbed the stairs to his bedroom to catch his cell ringing. When he picked it up, the face said *private.* Jun Tae frowned and set the phone back on the bedside table. He climbed onto the bed and tried getting comfortable. But the annoying phone calls from the private number were beginning to irritate him. The moment Fynn walked through the door, with a tray piled high with scrambled eggs, toast, two glasses of orange juice, steaming mugs of tea and fruits, Jun Tae couldn't focus on anything else.

"Oh Fynn."

"It's not much…" Fynn set the tray on the bed.

"This is perfect." Jun Tae kissed him before accepting one of the mugs. He took a quick sip. "Let's sit on the floor. It's a little bit more stable then the bed."

Fynn smiled and they moved everything to the hardwood floor at the foot of the bed.

With the sun coming up over Toronto, Jun Tae sat with this man and ate breakfast with his fingers. It was a simple meal but it was the best one he'd ever had. The laughter that was generated, the soft touches, the stolen kisses—everything about that moment in time was absolutely perfect. He couldn't remember the last time he laughed so hard, felt so necessary.

"Well, I've been thinking about the music video," Jun Tae said.

"Oh yeah?" Fynn bite into a banana.

"Yeah. *Love Me Like You Mean It* is a sexy song. The video has to match."

"You think?" Fynn asked. "I'm not afraid of a little bump and grind."

Jun Tae laughed. "I was hoping you'd say that because I was thinking you and I could be the lead in it."

Fynn watched him with that same slow,

unreadable expression as the day they'd met. Jun Tae covered his unease by lifting his juice to his lips.

"It was only a suggestion," Jun Tae said.

"You do realize this song is about two people who are so in love with each other, they can't keep their hands off each other? That this song is very sexual and the video, for it to have an impact will have to portray that and that chances are your parents and brother will see it?"

"You said it yourself. It's my happiness," Jun Tae whispered. "I'm claiming it and you. They made it perfectly clear they don't want to be in my life. And you're right, I can't keep living my life hoping they'll approve. I want to be happy. I want to love who I love, be who I am and flourish."

Fynn reached across to caress the side of

Jun Tae's face.

"You do things to me, Fynn and I want the world to know that if you'll have me, I'm yours."

Fynn smiled.

"And I've said too much too soon." Jun Tae pulled his face from his hand.

"Jun Tae Min…"

Jun stared at him. "That's my name. Don't wear it out."

Fynn laughed. "Didn't you hear a thing I said last night? I'm here. I'll be here for as long as you need me."

"So you don't mind if I start thinking of you as—well—as…"

"Spit it out, Jun."

"My man."

"Your man, eh?" Fynn looked thoughtful for a second before he grinned, pushed to his knees and kissed Jun Tae deeply. "I like the sound of that."

♥

Fynn closed the door to his car and jogged up the front steps of his parent's house with a bunch of flowers in one hand. He let himself into the foyer and removed his shoes. "Ma?"

When he got no answer, he followed the sound of laughter to the backyard to find his mother and father, sitting around, grilling and drinking wine.

"Happy birthday, Ma," Fynn said.

"Sweetheart!" Paulette cheered rising to hug him.

He offered her the flowers, accepted her affections before accepting a kiss to the side of the head from his father. "I thought they'd be others."

"Nope. Just us. I wanted to spend my birthday with my two favourite men." Paulette gathered a vase to put the flowers in. "But if you'd like to invite someone…"

"Me? Who would I invite?" Fynn asked.

"Your father tells me you've been spending a lot of time with this Jun Tae fellow," Paulette said. "We have yet to meet him."

Fynn smiled. He knew it was only a matter of time before the news reached his mother. He hadn't been trying to hide it but he didn't know if Jun Tae wanted everyone to know. Sure, Carson was cool with it but Fynn hadn't been certain of everyone else. "Well, let me call him and ask."

"Perfect!" Paulette said, clapping her

hands with glee. "I'll grab more steaks."

"Mom I don't know if he'll…" Fynn had to stop for the screen door slammed behind her as she disappeared into the house.

Denny laughed. "You know your mother, when it comes to your happiness there is no talking to her."

Fynn nodded and grabbed a bottle of water from the deck fridge. "He's really something amazing, dad. We've had a few performances around the city and now we're getting calls to perform at bigger shows."

"That's great." Denny dropped a steak on the grill. "Why don't you look impressed? I saw your Kingville performance and I thought it was amazing."

"Thanks. And I am impressed. Carson asked if we would like to become a duo. Jun Tae is scared that us being together all the time on stage will affect our personal relationship."

"It's a very sound concern."

"I wouldn't say sound." Fynn took a long drink from his water. "I mean, I like the guy. I will always fight to keep the public and stage separate."

Denny nodded. "Yes, good intentions and all that. How many Hollywood relationship breaks down because one is jealous of the other or the public and the media finds a way to worm their way into it? You two have to sit down and talk about this—about how you'll keep all that negativity out."

"I should call him."

"Sure, son. But listen to me. You seem to have a serious thing for this cat," Denny said, reaching for a beer. "Be smart about it. If you see the world is intruding in what you're trying to build, it's time to go dark like Jack Bauer, and fix things. Do not let the fame ruin things, neither you or him need the money."

"No. But we both need the music."

Denny raised his beer in a silent toast and Fynn excused himself while pulling out his cell. He called Jun Tae who didn't pick up on the first call but did on the second.

"Really? They want to meet me?" Jun Tae asked.

"Yeah. Look, you don't have to. This is only if you want to and you think you're ready."

"Yes! I mean, of course. I have to get your mother a gift then."

"Baby, you don't have to do that."

"Of course I do!" Jun Tae sounded as if he was rushing around the room.

"Look out for the…"

"Ouch! Damn it!"

"Chest." Fynn shook his head. Jun Tae seemed to always crash into the chest at the foot of his bed since he'd bought it only a few days before. "Jun, nothing is open right now."

"I'll find something."

"And bring a change of clothes. We're staying here tonight because of the drinking."

Jun Tae went silent. "They're not going to be weird and force us to sleep in separate rooms, are they?"

Fynn laughed. "No. I don't think my parents are under any delusions about what we do in the bedroom."

"Jerk."

But Fynn could hear laughter in Jun Tae's voice. "Would you like me to come pick you up? We could use a quiet few minutes alone before coming here. I could use a few minutes alone with you."

"I know we haven't really had time to spend together since this whole music thing plus the filming of the video…I'm sorry. We can't let the outside world intrude on us like this."

"You're right. How do you suggest we fix it?"

"I saw we book a certain number of gigs," Jun Tae said. "When those are finished we clear our schedules for two weeks and we go somewhere we can be alone. And we don't think of music or Carson."

"Just you and me?"

"Yup."

"Okay baby. Let me put my shoes on. I'll be at your place in twenty."

"See you soon, Trix."

Fynn grinned and hung up. That was the first time Jun Tae had used the nickname. It sound overly sexy leaving his lips.

"Ma! I'm going to leave for a bit." He called.

She stuck her head into the house. "Where are you going?"

"To pick up Jun Tae. I'll be back."

"Okay darling, drive safe."

Chapter Eight

Jun Tae met Fynn on the last floor and admitted him into the elevator up to the penthouse. The moment they were in through the door, Fynn had him against the wall, their mouths fused together, bodies crushing into each other's. He moaned, tangled his arms around Fynn's neck and leaned into the kiss as if his life depended on it.

"Hey," Jun Tae whispered.

"Hey yourself." Fynn kissed him again.

"We should go. Your parents must be

waiting."

"Kind of. They know about us so Ma won't mind." Fynn kissed him. "But you're right. If we start anything we'll not make it to the party."

Jun Tae laughed and extricated his body from Fynn. Though he wanted nothing more than to lead Fynn to his bedroom, he behaved and grabbed his things, including a bottle of wine he'd bought the first night in the condo. "Do you think she will like this?" Jun Tae asked. "It was late to stop and pick up anything else."

"Baby…"

"I didn't want to just show up with my two empty hands. It's rude."

Fynn sighed. "All right. It'll be fine. If you want to get her a present, she loves books and you can make it a belated birthday present—eh?"

Jun Tae felt better with that thought so he nodded. With Fynn's arm wrapped around his hips, they left the condo and wandered down to the visitor's parking lot. Jun Tae wondered if he could get a parking pass and spot for Fynn but he would ask the management office before he said anything to Fynn. It was a bit of a trek to the visitor's lot and he didn't want Fynn to have to do that every time.

He sighed as Fynn's large hand moved its way along the small of his back then up to his shoulder.

When they were on their way, Jun Tae turned to stare at Fynn. His strong cheekbones were set with a slight determination, and his brown eyes were glued to the road. Jun Tae remembered how they heated, and sparkled in bed and he smiled and looked away.

"I've dated a couple of guys before you," Jun Tae said. "And none of them made me as happy as you have already."

"Really?" Fynn asked without looking away from the road.

"Really."

"That's great to hear. I can't put all the blame for my unhappiness on them." Jun Tae sighed. "I was scared my parents would find out, afraid of the shame I would cause to descend on their house that I didn't even stop to enjoy the men I was with. They didn't stand a chance."

"That wasn't fair to them."

"You're right. But if I was fair to them I wouldn't have found you."

Fynn did glance at him then but only for a quick second.

"Fynn, I don't know where we're going.

But between the music and this—this—what we're doing, I'm happy."

"That's all you can hope for, Jun. Don't read too much into anything."

"Yeah."

Jun turned his attention back outside to the darkening world. The sun was going down between the trees leaving the sky with an unhealthy dose of orange flecks. The temperature dipped slightly as well. Though he didn't require a jacket, Jun Tae could feel the change in the air.

"I've been thinking of Carson said about the duet thing."

"Oh yeah?" Fynn asked.

"I think we should do it. But, in Korea bands work for years because they're allowed to do solo stuff so I'd like that option."

"I agree. So we do stuff together and on

our own." Fynn said, nodding. "I like that."

Jun Tae was never any more exhilarated. The thought of working side by side with Fynn to make music he loved, he had a hand in creating, was going to be something he'd cherish forever. At Fynn's place, he walked into the large house to music playing loudly. He arched a brow and followed Fynn to the backward where a couple was dancing.

He noticed the large smile on Fynn's lips and assumed they were his parents.

"Fynn!" Paulette cheered.

"Welcome back!" Denny said.

The two hurried over and Fynn turned to Jun Tae. "Ma, Dad, this is Jun Tae Min."

Jun Tae grinned and extended a hand but Paulette merely hugged him. Denny shook his hand though and the four sat around for dinner. They talked about everything from music to art to history and not one cross word was spoken even when someone disagreed with another. All of this was new to Jun Tae but he loved it. He loved the spirit that wrapped its arms around the backyard making it something he'd yearned for—the perfect imperfection of a family.

There was an adoration amongst them—Denny, Paulette and Fynn—a warmth and caring Jun Tae never experienced before. He smiled and lifted his drink to his lips to hide his wandering thoughts.

"You're staying the night, Jun Tae," Paulette was saying. "Fynn here's had wine."

"Yes, thank you, Mrs. Gibbs."

"Oh don't be so formal." Paulette rose and took Denny's hand. "Paulette is fine. Now, Denny and I are going to turn in. We have to make a couple of calls before we go to sleep so we're leaving you two boys."

Fynn laughed. He tilted his head and Paulette kissed his cheek so did Denny. Jun Tae accepted a pat on the shoulder from Denny and a wave from Paulette before they left the room hand in hand, speaking softly to each other.

"I get so jealous of you sometimes," Jun Tae said.

"Of me? Why?"

"Your parents are amazing," Jun Tae admitted. "My parents want me to fall off the face of the…"

He pulled his cell out and stared at the screen before dropping it back into his pocket.

"That's going to keep ringing."

Jun Tae shrugged. "I don't know who it is. They keep calling private and when I answer they say nothing."

Fynn nodded.

The phone stopped.

Silence.

The phone rang again.

Jun Tae growled and answered it. "Yes? Look, if you're going to keep calling you might as well say something! Hello? *Annyeonghseyo?*"

Fynn extended his hand and Jun Tae was about to hand over the phone when a small, trembling voice spoke. He didn't hear what it said.

"*Annyeong...*"

"Jun Tae, it's Won."

Jun Tae gasped. It'd been so long since he heard his brother's voice, every part of his body went still.

"Jun?" Fynn asked. "What's the matter?"

"Won—hi."

"I'm sorry I must seem like a stalker but I didn't know what to say and I needed to hear your voice."

"Does dad know you're calling?" Jun Tae asked.

"Yes."

"Won, you're going to lose everything."

"Too late for that." Won whispered. "But you're my brother and over the past few weeks I realize that even though I can live without my mother and father—I can't without my brother. I'm so sorry. *Nal yongseo haejwo.*"

"Forgive you? Won Bin for what?"

"You were everything to me," Won Bin said. "I should have been stronger. I should've known that even when the world falls apart you'd still be in my blood. I betrayed you because I was a coward and I'm sorry."

"Won Bin..." Jun Tae rose and walked away to stand at the railing. He stared out into the night and bowed his head. "Where are you?

Are you all right?"

"I'm at a hotel. I'll be okay."

"I'm sending someone to get you. Let me call you back."

"Jun Tae…"

"You can't stay there, Won. It's not safe."

"I will deserve what I get."

"That's not how it works!" Jun Tae growled. "You are my brother and you've left me once before! Do *not* even think you can do it again. Now, stay put. Text me your number and I will call you back."

"Okay…"

Jun Tae hung up and bowed his head.

"Talk to me," Fynn said. "What do you need from me?"

Jun Tae said nothing. He turned and pressed his face into Fynn's neck, inhaling his scent and finding courage in Fynn's arms as they wrapped around him. He remained where he was, silently, pulling himself together until his phone chirped. He checked the face to see Won Bin had texted him as he'd all but demanded. Once he saw that, he read the number out to himself, a way to commit them to memory and called Carson.

"JT! How's it going, brother?" Carson's big voice was husky with sleep.

"Hey. I need a favour."

"Sure. Don't see how much good I can do from here, but let's have it."

"My brother. He's in trouble and I need you to swing by and get him," Jun Tae said.

"But your brother and your parents…"

"He couldn't stay mad at me, Carson. Now he has nothing. I was lucky because I had my music and money saved but Won Bin went home to work with our father. He has nothing. Please…"

"All right, brother. Tell me where he is…"

Jun Tae made a few more call and a few hours later the plan was set. Carson would get Won Bin in Korea and bring him back to Toronto. There shouldn't be an issue with Won getting into the country due to his dual citizenship. Won Bin would stay with Jun Tae and they'd figure it out from there. But as the adrenaline began wearing off, Jun Tae saw the issue with that plan. He found Fynn sitting in the dark in his parent's living room.

"You know this ends when your brother gets here," Fynn said when Jun Tae reached the door.

"It doesn't have to."

"I really do think you believe that."

Fynn didn't move and in that moment, Jun Tae lost him in the darkness.

"I do believe it," Jun Tae said.

"Your brother is coming. He'll be staying with you."

"What did you want me to do, leave him there alone?" Jun Tae asked.

"He left you alone!" Fynn snapped. "He left you to wander Korea by yourself. He and your parents broke you almost to the core and the second he calls you go running! You throw away everything to go back to this guy who did that to you."

"He's my brother!"

"I get that!" Fynn snarled. "I get it but now you're doing to me the same thing he's done to you. You're leaving me alone."

"That's not fair!"

"Isn't it, Jun?" Fynn asked.

"I don't know why you thought I wouldn't help my brother!" Jun Tae shouted.

"Hey!" Denny thundered. "Hey! What is with the yelling!"

"Do you two know what time it is?" Paulette followed up.

"Sorry, Paulette," Jun Tae said.

But Fynn merely grabbed his keys and stormed out of the house. Jun Tae rubbed his eyes and hung his head.

"I'm sorry," he whispered. The sound of Fynn's car roared to life and soon disappeared in the distance. "I should go."

"Don't you wander out too," Denny said. "I'll go after him. You, stay here." He kissed Paulette and left.

"Come, I'll make you some tea."

Jun Tae wanted to argue. But he was so tired of conflict, so weak with exhaustion and just about finished with everything and everyone. He followed and climbed onto a stool.

"You want to tell me what got the two of you so worked up?" Paulette asked.

"My brother," Jun Tae replied. "When I came out my parents turned their backs on me and because my brother was afraid of losing everything he went with them. I guess his conscience is bothering him because now he tried to stand up for me and out parents did the same thing to him. I can't leave him in Korea by himself. He'd never last. He has no money, no home of his own, everything he had came from my father."

"The father giveth and the father taketh away."

"Yeah. I'm bringing him here and Fynn is not pleased."

"I see." Paulette said softly.

She poured some water over a peppermint bag and Jun Tae could smell the soothing aroma of the mint fill the kitchen.

"You know why he's angry, right?"

"At this point?" Jun Tae asked, accepting the mug. "I have no idea."

"Well, your relationship is over now," Paulette said. "To him, your brother won't be happy you're dating someone. He'll give you the ultimatum and before you know it, Fynn is out."

"That would never happen. My brother doesn't have that kind of hold on me anymore."

"No?" Paulette rested both her elbows on the counter and leaned forward. "Your brother hurt you in the worse possible way. Betrayal amongst siblings is often an unforgivable sin. Yet, your brother calls and you're off to the rescue."

"Damn. I'm sorry."

Paulette smiled and patted his shoulder. "Don't worry about it."

"Do you think Denny will find him?"

"Of course." Paulette smiled. "There's only one person on this planet who knows Fynn better than even Fynn—that's his father."

Jun Tae managed a sad smile more for Paulette than himself and took a sip from the peppermint. He ruminated on what Paulette had told him. Truth was, he hadn't thought of how Won Bin's arrival would affect his growing relationship with Fynn. Now that he was finally doing that, he couldn't help the searing shatter of his heart.

Chapter Nine

Fynn finished classes for the week and made his way to the studio. Carson had given him some time to work on some beats. Even though he hadn't spoken to Jun Tae in days, he figured since they did agree they would do solo stuff, he'd take the time to get a song pushed together for himself. He sat behind the boards with the beats playing a notepad in his lap and pen poised, waiting for inspiration to hit.

He wasn't sure how long he'd been sitting there but when he shook his head to clear it he had a whole song, the lyrics anyway, on the paper. He stopped the music, tweaked a few things, added a little bit more treble and restarted it.

Suddenly he knew he wasn't in the room alone, so he turned. Jun Tae was standing at the door with a man, his splitting image standing beside him. Fynn's heart raced and though he wanted to go back to that moment when he didn't know they were there, he knew he couldn't. Turning the music all the way down, he refocused on his lyrics.

"What do you want?" He asked.

"You can't keep hiding from me," Jun Tae said.

"Who's hiding? You know where I work, live, make music—where my parents live. Again, what do you want?"

"For one, I want to introduce my brother," Jun Tae said.

Fynn glanced over his shoulder at the young man by Jun Tae's said but didn't spare him a long look. "I have no intentions of meeting anyone in your family."

"Trix, you can't mean that." Jun Tae's voice trembled. "If this is going to work we have to get along with each other's family."

Fynn frowned. He dropped his notepad on the table beside him and turned in his seat. Draping his arms over the arms, he rested his gaze on Jun Tae's brother, the same man Jun had called Won Bin on the phone. "We have to get along?" Fynn asked. "Okay. I'm gay. I'm the man who's doing your brother. Can you live with that?"

Won Bin flinched.

"Didn't think so," Fynn said. "Thanks for stopping by, Jun. But you can take the poor out of man, it seems, but not the hate."

"You're hurting him," Won Bin said.

"And you didn't?" Fynn snapped. "Do you know what you and your parents did to him? You ripped his heart out all because he didn't fall into that neat little heterosexual package you have laid out for him. So don't you dare come in here and judge me."

"I don't care if he's gay!" Won Bin said. "You're just very vulgar—I've never heard anything like *I'm the man who's doing your brother* before. It's a little embarrassing to me. I'm sorry!"

Fynn growled.

"Fynn, please!" Jun Tae pleaded. "Please? The two of you are the men in my life who means more to me than I can ever imagine. You two have to get along."

Fynn dragged his right palm along the top of his head then down to the back of his neck. He licked his lips and turned his gaze back to Won Bin and Jun Tae. "I'm sorry, Jun. As much as I am falling for you, I can't be with with you and have a homophobic around. It wouldn't be...."

"But I'm not!" Won Bin declared. "You don't understand how things are back home. The kids don't live for themselves they live for the honour of their homes and their parent's name. I was scared and I did something unconscionable."

Jun Tae approached him and knelt between Fynn's thighs. "Darling, he really is trying. Give him a chance." He framed Fynn's cheeks with his hands. "For me."

There was no way Fynn could deny those eyes, those lovely brown eyes that saw so deeply into his soul. Weak, he bowed his head and dropped a kiss to Jun Tae's forehead. He then kissed him chastely against the lips.

"Okay." Fynn didn't break eye contact. "I'll give this a try for you. Only because you asked me too and I can think of no better way of showing you what I'm feeling for you."

"Thank you." Jun Tae eased upward for another quick kiss.

Fynn pressed his lips into a thin line and rose with Jun Tae. He rubbed his palms into the thighs of his pants to dry them before extended one to Won Bin.

"Won, this is Fynn Gibbs," Jun Tae said. "My boyfriend."

Fynn smirked.

"A pleasure to meet you, Fynn." Won Bin's voice cracked.

After that the ice was broken. Once Fynn allowed himself to relax around Won Bin and to think of the younger Min brother as less of a hindrance and more of someone who would be in his life, Fynn found he was able to relax more. They recorded the song, even had Jun Tae do some background work on it. When it was finished, Fynn could see the spark working on the music put in Won Bin.

"Do you sing?" Fynn asked.

"Who me?" Won Bin asked then laughed. "No. No way. No one has any interest in hearing me sing or rap. Jun got all that talent from the cosmos."

Jun Tae laughed. "That's true. Musicality does not run in the Min family."

"Well, any idea what you'll be doing?" Fynn asked. "Sooner or later you will get bored and start ripping your hair out."

"It's started already," Won Bin leaned in to confide. "I'm going stark raving mad staying in that condo. I was debating going back to school. I do have a little money saved up from working with dad."

"Oh yeah? What would you take?" Jun Tae asked.

"I like Marketing," Won Bin replied.

"Won Bin, listen," Fynn said. He inhaled and exhaled. "What I said earlier—about being the one who—well, you know? It was out of line and I'm sorry."

"I understand your frustration," Won Bin said. "It's okay. I shouldn't have reacted the way I did to Jun Tae coming out. I always knew there was a part of him he wasn't sharing with me and when he finally did, I should've manned up and did what's right."

"You were scared."

"No excuse," Won Bin said.

"Okay, you two," Jun Tae said, rubbing Fynn's back. "Enough of that. We're good—

it'll be all right. You'll see."

It took some doing but after a few hours, they left the studio, dropped Won Bin off at the condo then continued on to meet with Carson. It was time to turn on the fire under the career they'd been trying to build. When they climbed from the car, Jun Tae reached for his hand. They entered the office building like that, fingers interlaced.

"Guys!" Carson said. "What do you think of the new place?"

Fynn laughed. "Very nice!" The two bumped fists and Carson and Jun Tae hugged.

"Right? Come into my office."

They followed Carson down a short corridor and into an office that rivaled any high powered CEO. Glass walls, potted plants, leather chairs, mahogany desk—it was lovely. The three sat down over coffee and sandwiches and Carson threw so much information at them, Fynn felt as if his mind would explode.

"Okay so the first thing I need to do is add you two to the company's Youtube channel." Carson continued. "Over the next little while, there will be a videographer filming your performances on stage."

"Nothing else?" Jun Tae asked.

"No." Carson wiped his fingers into a paper napkin. "I know how you two feel about that. So just the stage. Also, we need to do is release a lyric video," He found a few nice ones on Youtube and showed them to Fynn and Jun Tae. "This gives a little bit of anticipation for the upcoming actual video."

"Those are nice," Fynn said. "I'll get the lyrics for you soon."

They went on to cover contracts as well. After all, though they were friends, business was business. By the time the meeting was over, it was late.

"I'll drop you home to your brother," Fynn said.

"I was hoping we could spend some time together."

"It would have to be at my place," Fynn told him. "I still find it a bit weird with your brother…"

"That's why you haven't touched me in days…"

Fynn sighed and took Jun Tae's hand. "Yes and I was mad at you."

"Are you still mad at me?" Jun Tae asked, pouting handsomely at Fynn.

Fynn trembled. "How can I be crossed at that face?"

"Well, you can apologize by taking me home." Jun Tae lifted Fynn's hand and dragged his lips against the back. "This shirt I'm wearing is really old—it rips very nicely if you try."

Fynn laughed softly and wrapped an arm around Jun Tae as they headed for the car. "You know, I'm getting the feeling you've always been a freak."

"Always? I have no idea what you're referring to, Fynn. I was innocent until you corrupted me."

"Wait, wait, wait." Fynn stopped and met his gaze. "I dare you to say that with a straight face."

"I don't take dares," Jun Tae sputtered, lifting his chin.

Fynn could see the beginning of a grin lighting up Jun Tae's face as Jun Tae walked away.

"A-ha!" Fynn cheered. "You a freak!"

"I categorically deny that!" Jun laughed.

Fynn jogged after his boyfriend singing Adina Howard's *Freak Like Me.*

Epilogue

Two years later and somehow, Jun Tae and Fynn managed to pull their lives together and onward. Jun Tae was still nervous about what they were about to do but when he told Fynn, his boyfriend merely grinned that beautiful grin and said, "don't worry Sexy Thang! I got you."

Jun Tae trusted Fynn with everything but his heart still raced as people around him ran to and fro through last minute preparations.

What always surprised Jun Tae when they performed in Korea, was the way the fans were with him. When they knew he was next, they would started chanting the group's name—JT & Gibbs—over and over until the first set of pyro went off on stage. Then everyone shrieked so loud, the noise became like a dull hum.

Still, stopped just out of view of the audience, curled his fingers against the back of Fynn's neck and pressed their foreheads together. As usual, he whispered a prayer only he and Fynn could hear before opening his eyes. He waited for Fynn to kiss his forehead, between his eyes then his lips. For some reason, Jun Tae couldn't seem to take the stage without those tender brushes of his lover's lips.

"I love you," Fynn whispered to him. "I wanted you to know that."

Jun Tae floated out of himself and off into the clouds. After a year of dating and working and struggling through relationship highs and lowers, he couldn't believe those words had left Fynn's lips.

"Say that again."

"I love you."

Jun Tae grinned widely. "I love you too!" He kissed Fynn again just as the announcer shouted their names.

"Go!" Won Bin hollered.

Laughing, Jun Tae accepted the microphone someone offered and walked underneath the stage to the platform. He glanced over to see Fynn doing the same. When Fynn winked at him, Jun Tae's knees wobbled under him. Still, he had just enough time to blow Fynn a kiss before the platform began moving upward. He and Fynn kept their eyes locked onto each other for as long as they could before they shot up onto the stage and into the air. When they landed, the platform had become a part of the stage, keeping them up.

And with that, another concert began. This was their first major one and when Carson suggested it, Jun Tae thought he was crazy. There was no way they could sell out an arena. People hated Jun Tae—didn't they? Jun Tae counted down to the day tickets went on sale for everyone. On the day, he and Fynn were in the middle of making love but the phone just wouldn't stop ringing. Irritated, he rolled away from Fynn and answered it.

"You guys did it!" Carson cheered. "You sold out the arena in two hours, brother!"

One song blended into another. They even took breaks to speak to the audience. Though Fynn had learned some Korean, he still needed some translation help but the audience loved every second of it. When it was over, they went back onstage for two encores until

Jun Tae said no to the third. He could see how exhausted Fynn had been.

When they were finally back at the hotel, they made love again and Fynn fell asleep. Jun Tae sat with his back against the headboards, looking down into his face wondering how in the world he'd gotten so lucky. Fynn Gibbs was a good man, an amazing mad. He was tender, loving and had to be crazy because he loved Jun Tae.

Jun Tae smoothed a hand over his head and leaned into press a kiss to his ear. "I love you too, Fynn Gibbs—more than I thought I was capable of."

Sure, Jun Tae's parents hadn't come around. Hell, they may never come around. But he couldn't help the happiness that floated through him like a flower blooming. As he shifted to lay behind Fynn and kiss his back before wrapping an arm around him, Jun Tae understood what true contentment meant. It meant having love in his life—not many people loving him, but quality people loving him. It meant having his brother by his side and Fynn Gibbs in his bed, career and heart.

"I love you, Fynn Gibbs," Jun Tae said.

Fynn turned in the circle of Jun Tae's arms then with his beautiful, brown eyes full of sleep and desire. He cradled the side of Jun Tae's face and smiled, causing the corners of his lush lips to tug upward. "I love you too, baby."

The End

ABOUT THE AUTHOR

Writing romance for one special girl…

Printed in Great Britain
by Amazon